THE MEAT TREE

GWYNETH LEWIS

THE MEAT TREE

NEW STORIES FROM THE

MABINOGION

SEREN

To Eira

Seren is the book imprint of
Poetry Wales Press Ltd
57 Nolton Street, Bridgend, Wales, CF31 3AE
www.seren-books.com

© Gwyneth Lewis 2010

ISBN 978-1-85411-523-2

A CIP record for this title is available from the British Library.

This book is a work of fiction. The characters and incidents por-
trayed are the work of the author's imagination. Any other resem-
blance to actual persons, living or dead, is entirely coincidental.

Cover design by Mathew Bevan

Inner design and typesetting by books@lloydrobson.com

Printed in the Czech Republic by Akcent Media Ltd

The publisher acknowledges the financial support of the
Welsh Books Council.

Contents

New Stories from the Mabinogion

Introduction

Some stories, it seems, just keep on going. Whatever you do to them, the words are still whispered abroad, a whistle in the reeds, a bird's song in your ear.

Every culture has its myths; many share ingredients with each other. Stir the pot, retell the tale and you draw out something new, a new flavour, a new meaning maybe. There's no one right version. Perhaps it's because myths were a way of describing our place in the world, of putting people and their search for meaning in a bigger picture that they linger in our imagination.

The eleven stories of the *Mabinogion* ('story of youth') are diverse native Welsh tales taken from two medieval manuscripts. But their roots go back hundreds of years, through written fragments and the unwritten, storytelling tradition. They were first collected under this title, and translated into English, in the nineteenth century.

The *Mabinogion* brings us Celtic mythology, Arthurian romance, and a history of the Island of Britain seen through the eyes of medieval Wales – but tells tales that stretch way beyond the boundaries of contemporary Wales, just as the 'Welsh' part of this island once did: Welsh was once spoken as far north as Edinburgh. In one tale, the gigantic Bendigeidfran wears the crown of London, and his severed head is buried there, facing France, to protect the land from invaders.

There is enchantment and shape-shifting, conflict, peacemaking, love, betrayal. A wife conjured out of flowers is punished for unfaithfulness by being turned into an owl, Arthur and his knights chase a magical wild boar and its piglets from Ireland across south Wales to Cornwall, a prince changes places with the king of the underworld for a year...

Many of these myths are familiar in Wales, and some have filtered through into the wider British tradition, but others are little known beyond the Welsh border. In this series of New Stories from the Mabinogion the old tales are at the heart of the new, to be enjoyed wherever they are read.

Each author has chosen a story to reinvent and retell for their own reasons and in their own way: creating fresh, contemporary tales that speak to us as much of the world we know now as of times long gone.

Penny Thomas, series editor

The structure of every organic being is related, in the most essential yet often hidden manner, to that of all other organic beings, with which it comes into competition for food or residence, or from which it has to escape, or on which it preys.

Charles Darwin, *The Origin of Species*

The Meat Tree

1

Technical Preparation

Synapse Log 28 Jan 2210, 09:00

Inspector of Wrecks

Is that working now, I wonder? I hate these thought recorders. They're good in very confined spaces, where you don't want to overhear the idiotic things your colleagues say to their families back on Mars, but I think they're overrated. But, there we are, I'm Old School. The trick is to keep the unconscious out of it as much as possible and pretend that you're talking to yourself.

Now, I think it's settling down. Right. Well, we're just about approaching the Mars Outer Satellite Orbit. Not seeing too much debris around at the moment, they must have had a clean up fairly recently. Last time I was here, you could hardly move for junk. We've glimpsed the ship in the distance, and should arrive later this afternoon.

The new girl's feeling sick but won't admit it. She thinks I don't know that she threw up in the heads, but you can't hide any smells in a spacecraft. If Nona doesn't stop vomiting, I'll have to make her take the drugs. Her eyes are red already, she's dehydrated. I can't have her out of action, we're too close to the target vessel. Typical, getting lumbered with a student on my last mission.

Before anything starts happening, I'm going to get my expenses software set up...

Apprentice
So Campion's telling me how he does his mileage first 'and all else follows' and I'm about to throw up all over him, but I manage to swallow it. Ironic. My whole life to get into Mars orbit, and now I'm here I feel too awful to take it in.

I did get to look out of a porthole as we passed close to home. Saw a dust storm in Thaumasia, thousands of miles wide. It looked like miso soup when you stir it up. Made me nauseous all over again.

So I stopped looking. You wouldn't believe how hard it is to catch floating vomit in a paper bag.

We're not one day in and I'm already tired of hearing about the Department of Wrecks in the Good Old Days. When flotsam came in from as far as the Sculptor galaxy or the Microscopium Void. When he had a full team and they got to work on really interesting cultures. Not like this speck from God knows where, just me and him – the one man in the service who has absolutely no imagination.

Oh, I think he wants to do an equipment check.

Joint Thought Channel 28 Jan 2210, 09:02

Inspector of Wrecks
This is so that we can talk to each other on the vessel without disturbing any of the artifacts. Sometimes alien communication patterns can be diffused by the human voice, so we'll keep to Joint Thought mode until we know more about what's going on.

Apprentice
You mean like a mind-meld? God! I didn't mean to say that.

Inspector of Wrecks
The whole trick of this channel is to avoid personal static.
Keep it professional.

Apprentice
Sorry. Of course.

Inspector of Wrecks
It's a knack. Not a silent version of speaking out loud, but
it's a way of sharing two sets of sense impressions from
slightly different angles. It doubles the amount of data we
can record. But you'll have to learn to make a very precise
form of running commentary. It's not your uncensored
thoughts, but it's not formal reporting either. Try doing it on
me for a second.

Apprentice
He looks much taller than he did on Mars. And skinnier.

Inspector of Wrecks
That's close, but you can do better. It's a question of what's
appropriate. Give me some sensory data, because that's often
much more valuable than your opinions. We won't know what
we're seeing, but we need to record the effect it's having on
us. Try again.

Apprentice
The smell of his soap makes me sick to my stomach, I can't get away from it.

Inspector of Wrecks
That's much, much better. Relevant stuff. A little personal, perhaps, but that's good. We'll be getting all the objective data from the robots we send in before us.

    Again.

Apprentice
His comb-over looks like the tendrils of a plant in zero gravity.

Inspector of Wrecks
That's it, you're getting it. And don't worry, you can't offend me. What I'm looking for is information. Record it, even if it doesn't seem important at the time. I'm particularly interested in alien emotio-translation technology, we have a lot to learn in that area. This technique is going to be especially important if we have to go into Virtual Reality.

Apprentice
The sleep of leaves!

Inspector of Wrecks
All right! That's it! That will do for now. Oh, and I'll change the soap. Didn't realise it was a problem. You should have said.

2

Approach

Synapse Log 28 Jan 2210, 15:00

Inspector of Wrecks

Could never understand why so many people find space travel boring. There's nothing like the excitement of being out in deep space, watching volcanic plumes rise over Io in Jupiter-shine. Or seeing an asteroid pass like a piece of pumice, or like one of those ancient Henry Moore sculptures, torsos without limbs. Don't suppose she has the faintest idea who Henry Moore was, she's far too young. They don't learn even the basics these days…

Just off Mars and we're practically home, I can see my dome near the rippled flats of Argyre Planitia. It was snowing when we passed last time.

Apprentice

The way we approach the vessel, slow and steady, I love it. Last time I looked, the target ship was the size of the moon on my fingernail. Now it's an eye, coming closer, looking at us with curiosity.

He

Just my luck. It looks like a fairly primitive mid-Carolingian solar sailing vessel. Two rings of concave photon sails, maybe Mylar and Kapton, a habitat module like the stigma of a flower. In fact, the whole thing looks like a daffodil. Pity. You've seen one of these, you've seen them all. No chance now of my adding anything spectacular to my life list. It's a bog-standard rudimentary Earth vessel.

She

Been hailing them for hours. The old fart gave me the signals job, but the modem's tried all the inter-galactic space languages and no response.

We've just gone under the shadow of one of the solar arrays. I've heard about these old-style ships, but never seen one before. Billions and billions of photons slam into the sail and nudge the vessel backwards. Crude, but effective. If this came from Earth, they might have combined it with that gravity-sling technique they used for a while.

It's eerie in the shadow of the heliogyro. Can't tell if we're being watched or not. As if the old sight lines have worn a groove in space. Fanciful, I know. It could be centuries since anybody boarded this vessel, but still I can feel the tug of those eyes.

Campion stood us down till tomorrow morning, so that we're fresh for the boarding. Gave me his old manual to read, as if I was interested in that antique and didn't have sub-eyelid protocols to study for my exams. Suppose I'd better look at it so as to humour the old man. After all, we're going to be within fifteen feet of each other while this trip lasts, so let's keep it sweet.

He

I love this part, getting my equipment prepared, not knowing exactly what we're going to find on board. You've got to be ready for anything. And a little bit scared that you won't be up to the challenge.

I just can't believe that they're suspending Wreck Inspections by humans and trusting that remote viewing rubbish. You need the human touch in trying to figure out what went wrong on these voyages, especially if they're alien in origin. A computer programme just won't get it and we'll learn nothing from the flotsam that's coming right to our doorstep. It's a treasure trove. What a criminal waste.

Sure, they're giving the girl some basic wreck training with me, but she's a technician and just hasn't got the cultural expertise to know what she's seeing. She seems nice enough – was even interested in my old manual – but they're basically flushing the culture of space travel out with the body fluids.

And what am I going to do in that horrible station on Mars? No, don't think about that now. Enjoy this voyage while it lasts. Think about dying later.

She

I mean, look at this stuff. It's so old it's quaint:

> The high frontier represents an evolutionary departure in human culture that requires the

merging of art and science, economics and technology, public and private sectors in the pursuit of free enterprise and human enrichment.

Ra-ra or what! And the headings: 'Dress and Appearance of Humans and Robots Aloft', 'High Offworld Performance', 'Crew Prototypes of the Future', 'Lunar Industrialisation Possibilities'. And listen to this:

Initially, the focus should be upon human performance, productivity, crew team morale and management for long-term space living, including *stress reduction*. Special programmes, some computerised, will be developed to counteract the negative effects of an isolated, confined environment and lifestyle. Eventually it will extend to the role of other animals who are introduced into space habitats and settlements.

When he was young they were still carting stock round the universe, as if you couldn't grow any animal or vegetable tissue you wanted from stem

GWYNETH LEWIS

cells. Just think of those early dogs and monkeys in orbit. Barbaric. Better not tell him that, I suppose. So easy to offend a person, especially a dinosaur like him. They get cranky in old age. Perhaps I could say something nice about the 'Epilogue: Space Light', which is very poetic.

And I was hoping that this assignment would be fun.

3

Boarding

Joint Thought Channel 29 Jan 2210, 09:00

Inspector of Wrecks
We're in!

Apprentice
Breathe slowly, breathe. Try not to show how frightened you are.

Inspector of Wrecks
No disgrace in that. You'd be a fool not to be nervous at this stage. Just concentrate on moving slowly and noticing as much as you can. Now that we're out of the lock, why don't you take over?

Apprentice
How come he's breathing so slowly, as if he were taking a stroll in the park?

Inspector of Wrecks
Don't shine it on me. Look around you. Break it down.

Apprentice
Our lights are like columns, picking out the desks of a tiny control room. Atmosphere's dense with motes.

Inspector of Wrecks
Now you're getting the hang of it. What more? Don't be afraid of being subjective, but don't clutter the narrative.

Apprentice
By the design, the module looks like one of those retro twenty-second-century probes. But it can't be… there are space-shuttle touches, like the two-way switches they had to move manually before command functions were internalised. Look at this! You had to really mean it to switch this back and forth.

Inspector of Wrecks
This isn't retro. It's the real thing. Look at these mother-boards, they're huge!

Apprentice
That doesn't make sense. Space technology this primitive

could never have reached here from Earth. This thing belongs in a museum. What is that?

Inspector of Wrecks
No, it can't be. I've heard old-timers talking about something like this, but I've never seen one. I think it's something called an audio-cassette player. There's even a tape in it. Early personal entertainment system.

Apprentice
You're kidding, when technology was still outside the body! That's hilarious.

Inspector of Wrecks
See those couches? I bet they're old VR systems.

Apprentice
VR?

Inspector of Wrecks
Virtual Reality. Before you swallowed the nano-synaptic dream tablets for training and recreation.

Apprentice
Clunky or what!

Inspector of Wrecks
This whole ship's an anachronism, there's no way it could have survived the journey… and yet the bot says that the atmosphere's inhabitable. Well, we might as well start finding out.

Right. Watch me carefully. This is one of the most important moments in any investigation. I'm going to take off my helmet and start breathing the ship's own atmosphere. We know it's not going to kill me, but this first intake of breath can tell you a lot, if you know what you're looking for. Pay attention.

Apprentice
So methodical. Gauntlets first, helmet second. Like taking off his head.

Inspector of Wrecks
With the first breath, I can never be sure what I'm taking in. The dust of dead bodies. Toxins. Viruses. The gas from new life forms. One of the things I'm trying to scent is fear, and I often find it.

Apprentice
Stands there like a dog smelling food on the wind.

Inspector of Wrecks
Shush, I need quiet.

Apprentice
*Or like a sommelier, tasting the bouquet of a space vessel.
Very sophisticated.*

Inspector of Wrecks
*Please! You never get that first impression again, your nose
becomes accustomed to the background scent in a couple of
minutes. If you chat, it's wasted.*

Apprentice
Sorry.

Inspector of Wrecks
*Now you have a go. Don't think, but open your brain to
the scent molecules on board. What do you get?*

Apprentice
I don't know...

Inspector of Wrecks
Yes, your body does...

Apprentice
Can it be? Flowers?

Inspector of Wrecks
What else?

Apprentice
Flowers. And meat.

4

Entry

Synapse Log 29 Jan 2210, 20:30

Apprentice

End of a long day. Boarding was exciting, but after that Campion had me combing through the voyage log – paper, for Chrissakes! – looking for anything unusual, while he poked around the habitat module. I've had to drag out the grapho-palaeography from the back of my brain and try to make sense of the script.

But it's basically *nada*. Nothing unusual, everything as you would expect.

Inspector of Wrecks

I never expected to see one of these early Earth exploration vessels and in such a perfect state of preservation. It's like something in a museum. Even the hammocks are intact, as if someone just got up out of them and left them warm.

Missie's been moaning about having to decipher the ship's log, it's a history lesson for her. It'll do her good to see how space travellers in the past had to work, how uncomfortable it was.

Something's not right, though. It's all too perfect.

She

My print reading's crap but I managed to decipher that the vessel had a crew of three. One woman, two men. That must have been challenging in the days before phero-dampeners. Hard enough working with a man when we're both shielded from each other's body chemistry. Two men and one woman, must have been a recipe for disaster. What *did* they get up to?

He

Where are the bodies? Not even three piles of dust for us to analyse. No sign of forced exit, no breach in the spacecraft's hull. Nothing for us to go on.

She

And why can't we find any personal logs? Why they thought I had to do this one voyage the old-fashioned way, I don't know, it'll be irrelevant to everything else I do.

He

That ship's such a classic, it's like something out of the manual. The paper log and the black box show nothing out of the ordinary, and yet something devastating happened on board. And then there's the mystery of how a vessel designed for short-haul travel ended up millions of light years from Earth. Think, think. Something's staring us in the face but we're not seeing it…

She

Can't keep my eyes open. Even that noisy reactor isn't going to keep me awake tonight. What's that scratching on the hull? Must be bits of meteorites. I'm sure I can see flashes of particles passing through my eyelids…

He

I know! The VR couches! Right in the middle of the main cabin. They must have valued them highly to place the equipment so prominently. There may be some information to be gathered there. It's a big ask for the new girl to adapt to a strange VR, but what an education for her! Besides, she's quick on the uptake. Tomorrow, I'll take her in.

★

Joint Thought Channel 30 Jan 2210, 09:00

Inspector of Wrecks
Now, remember, if you feel uncomfortable at all, just raise your hand and we'll get out of the Virtual Reality Field immediately. The Escape button's in your right glove. The important thing to recall is that this is just fantasy. There's nothing in the programme that can hurt us, however realistic it looks at the time. Mind you, given how old this ship is, I expect the FX will be very crude.

Apprentice
All right, all right. I expect it's no different from the neuro games we play now.

Inspector of Wrecks
Hard to tell exactly what we're dealing with until we're in. The field could be anything. You're not claustrophobic, are you? If you are, let's note it in the Hazard log.

Apprentice
No. I'll be fine.

Inspector of Wrecks
These old VR helmets can be quite uncomfortable. But it's more than that. We're used to VR forming itself automatically to our frontal-lobe profiles, so that it responds to our particular fantasy life. But when the technology started, they still had one person author the programmes, so that being inside you're more a witness than co-creator. You have to take one of the available roles, but the parameters are set by the Mastermind. So the progression of the plot can feel very uncomfortable, especially if you're not used to it. And until we find out what kind of author we're dealing with it's hard to know what it will be like.

Apprentice
I'm sure I can manage.

Inspector of Wrecks
Atta girl! But if you don't like what's going on, remember the signal. We'll have to make a quick decision about which role to play. Watch what I do and we should be all right. Are you ready? Helmets on!

Right. What have we here? Looks like your basic medieval quest narrative.

Apprentice
Look at those colours! I love those greens and the intricate woodland plants.

Inspector of Wrecks
Hm. Earth vegetation. Sorrel, yarrow…

Apprentice
It smells aromatic.

Inspector of Wrecks
Forget the details for now. Let's try to get the big picture. Do you see that group of people over there, outside the castle walls? Can you make your way towards them?

Apprentice
Oops! Sorry, didn't mean to bump into you. The motility

software's really primitive.

Inspector of Wrecks
This takes me back to my boyhood! I used to play with my grandfather's antique games: they were just like this. Use the console in your left glove. That's better, much better. Right, I think you're ready to approach the group. And remember, you'll need to switch into one character's point of view.

Apprentice
Like one of those early avatar games?

Inspector of Wrecks
Yes, a bit. Except remember that you're not in control of your own character. The story's been written by the Mastermind. I'm not being sexist here, but why don't you see if you can take the role of the woman there who's kneeling in front of the blond man who looks like the king?

Apprentice
Got it!

My name is Goewin and I'm the footholder to King Math. I'm a virgin and very beautiful.

Inspector of Wrecks
I'm going for the character on the left, the one holding a staff. Give me a second.

   Right, I'm in. I'm Gwydion, a magician, and this is my brother Gilfaethwy.

Apprentice
Why has everything stalled?

Inspector of Wrecks
Don't worry, I think the software's just taking a moment to catch up with our choices. Use the time to learn what you can about your persona.

Apprentice
That's weird! The king's got his feet in my lap. They're quite heavy. Math is the Lord of a kingdom called Gwynedd.

Inspector of Wrecks
From the names, I'd say that we're in one of those old Celtic fantasies. In the early days of VR they were all the rage, I don't know why. It was fashionable to imagine yourself as a Welsh wizard or a Celtic maiden. Actually, you look very fetching in your costume.

Apprentice
It's velvet and my torque is gold.

Inspector of Wrecks
But why are you cradling the king's feet? Are his toes cold?

Apprentice
Don't be disrespectful. It's a special condition of the character. Math will die unless he has his feet in the lap of a virgin. So I'm the one keeping the king alive. The only time that he's allowed to touch the earth is when Gwynedd's at war.

Inspector of Wrecks
What a strange arrangement. Now it's quite important that we notice what's being said by these characters. I don't mean verbally but metaphorically. It's all information. Especially the initial briefs we're given, as they're full of primary significance. What are you told about this strange job you have?

Apprentice
I think it's to do with the king having to stay in touch with the magical fertility of his land. Though I don't understand it. A virgin's not fertile, is she?

Inspector of Wrecks
Only potentially. But it rings a bell. It's something to do with matriarchy, that the king is at the mercy of female sexuality. When I was a teenager, I read quite a bit of Robert Graves.

Apprentice
Who?

Inspector of Wrecks
Poet and mythologist. He wrote about the Goddess, who was deposed by patriarchal religion. Fascinating. This VR Field may be much earlier than I previously thought if it's using an image of the Goddess right in the Dramatis Personae.

Apprentice
The what?

Inspector of Wrecks
Surely you know... oh, never mind. The list of characters.

Apprentice
So I'm a goddess. All right!

Inspector of Wrecks
Not quite. You're her representative.

Apprentice
But you could just as easily read this differently. That the king is radically divorced from his land. What's the point of being king, if you can't have the pleasure of taking off your shoes and feeling the lush grass under your feet?

Inspector of Wrecks
So, what to make of two bodies together, like an uncopulating but coupled animal? Your position looks quite bizarre. Does it feel sexual? The early myths rarely were. They're much more about nature than sophisticated court mores. Nature's rarely sexy. It's only once you've moved one step away from the land that eroticism comes in. That's Eliade, if I remember rightly. Ever heard of Eliade?

Apprentice
Who?

Inspector of Wrecks
Never mind.

Apprentice

OK. I see. Yes, Math and I are stuck together, like man and wife, except that there's no hanky panky. Strictly platonic. Though I'm the most ravishing woman of my generation. Must be quite tricky for the king. That's all I have here. Except that I'm totally devoted to Math and feel that it's nothing but an honour to dedicate my life to keeping him alive.

Inspector of Wrecks

Interesting. Because I wouldn't have expected a…

Apprentice

Look, instead of showing off what you know, why don't you find out about your own character? I'm sorry, I didn't mean to…

Inspector of Wrecks

That's what being footholder to the king does for you. Gives you a certain haughtiness! You're beginning to play your part.

Apprentice

It's as though I'm starting to hear Goewin's tone of voice.

*You'd better hurry and catch up, I think this programme's
ready to roll.*

Inspector of Wrecks
*Right, back to basics. I'm Gwydion and the chap standing
next to me is my brother Gilfaethwy. I don't want to scare
you, but I think my brother has a passion for you.*

Apprentice
And should that worry me?

Inspector of Wrecks
*It should if you're wanting to stay a virgin. What he has in
mind is not medieval courting or holding hands.*

Apprentice
*Seems to me that I'm all right as long as the king's around.
And he'll only move if the kingdom's at war.*
    What are your qualities?

Inspector of Wrecks
I'm a magician and poet: the best storyteller in the world.

Apprentice
*Sounds like a much more useful skill than being the king's
footholder.*

Inspector of Wrecks
I wonder if this Gwydion is a shadow persona for the Mastermind of this whole VR. They often gave themselves a secondary character, so that they were both authors of the game and actors in them.

Apprentice
You mean like writing a story about themselves? And what's Gwydion like?

Inspector of Wrecks
Very clever. An escape artist with words. His big skill is that he's able to persuade other people to do things against their will. Oh, and he's sneaky. The type of man who pays his way with other people's suffering. And he'll do anything for his brother.

Apprentice
Oh my God! No!

Inspector of Wrecks
What's going on? Nona!

Apprentice
Get him off me! No!

Inspector of Wrecks
Shit! Something's gone wrong. It's a VR surge. Must be because this programme hasn't played for so long. It's going too fast. Oh! That strobe is terrible, I can't stand it.

Apprentice
The smell of him!

Inspector of Wrecks
Nona! Get out! Time to go. Remember the Escape switch!

Apprentice
In the king's own bed! Oh!

Inspector of Wrecks
Nona! Right glove! Press it now!

Apprentice
Oh! Thank God!

Inspector of Wrecks
What happened? Are you all right?

Apprentice
I thought you said that this was primitive VR, that nothing bad could happen to me in it.

Inspector of Wrecks
That's what I thought. It's from the same period as the ship.

Apprentice
Well he raped me. Gilfaethwy raped me. And it really hurt.

Inspector of Wrecks
But the technology shouldn't be able to do that. You saw, we only had on helmets and upper-body suits.

Apprentice
Don't tell me what did or didn't happen. I didn't have a chance. That bastard did it and you set it up.

Inspector of Wrecks
Something very strange is going on here. I don't understand it. We must have hit a crease in the field, because these stories are meant to unfold logically. But while you were screaming, I was seeing these crazy flash frames. Pigs from the Underworld. Magic stallions and hounds with gold saddles and leashes, all made from toadstools. Then out-and-out war between the South and Math. That must be why you were alone. Didn't you say that Math could only walk the ground when his kingdom was at war?

Apprentice
Fuck the story. I really don't care. Look at these bruises. These are real. VR shouldn't be able to do that.

Inspector of Wrecks
No, you're right. Perhaps the programme's faulty. I'll take a look at your suit before we go in again.

Apprentice
Again? Are you crazy? I didn't sign up for this, to be raped by a hairy medieval gangster.

Inspector of Wrecks
But it's…

Apprentice
Don't tell me it's fiction, that was something else. Why didn't you stop him?

Inspector of Wrecks
But he was my brother. And I'd promised to help.

I'm sure that if we'd let it run, I could have stopped it. After all, if I'm Gwydion, and if I understand my powers correctly, I should be able to get us out of any kind of situation like that.

Apprentice
But Gwydion planned it! You're my boss and you should be looking after me, not setting me up to be sexually assaulted.

Inspector of Wrecks
I'm sorry. I don't know why I said that, I seem to be still in character. Of course, you're right.

As with any self-teaching programme, as we go on, we have more control over our characters. That's been true from even the earliest days of VR.

Apprentice
I don't know…

Inspector of Wrecks
Look, sleep on it and see how you feel tomorrow. You've had a scare. Just put this down to experience.

Apprentice
I keep telling you, that was a real rape.

Inspector of Wrecks
I'll give you the code for some narco-oblivion meds. You'll be as right as rain in the morning. I promise.

Apprentice
I don't like taking that stuff, but I suppose…

Inspector of Wrecks
That's a good girl. And I'll do some work on the suit and its reality parameters. I promise you nothing like that will happen again. I'll make sure it doesn't.

5

Forest

Synapse Log 1 Feb 2210, 08:45

Inspector of Wrecks

I think the key to this is going to be identifying the Mastermind. I have a feeling it's Gwydion. He's the best storyteller in the world, a poet and wizard. What could be a clearer image for an early VR programmer? And if it *is* him I'm in a good position to delve further into the field's hinterland and perhaps find out what happened between the members of the ship's crew. After all, if they used VR a lot, then events are bound to have shaped the stories inside.

I hope Nona's all right. She's been very quiet.

Apprentice

If anything like that happens again and he tells me it was just VR, I'll kill him. And I don't mind telling him to his face if I have to.

He

I don't like to say anything, but she hasn't talked to me since the day before yesterday.

She

You can't just shove people into a VR field at the mercy of God knows what kind of Mastermind and expect them to bear it. If it were he who'd been abused, then he'd take it seriously.

He

Mind you, I think she started to come round when I said that she should take the part of Gwydion for the next visit. Then she can be sure that nothing will happen against her will.

She

If it were up to me, I'd go nowhere near that VR again. But he's fixated on it, and he's the boss.

He

That long chat last night helped a lot, when I took her through the work I'd done on the body suits. I like to think that some old-fashioned patience and reassurance made all the difference.

She

I'm beginning to see why they're phasing out these individual Inspectors. They spend much too much time on their own, making up stuff about what they find. They're bonkers. He's the most eccentric man I've ever met. He doesn't even use his channeller to help get him off to sleep. I've seen him *reading*. The man's not in the real world.

He

The human touch. It's what these youngsters are lacking. Once she saw the logic of going back in, she was with me.

She

Bloody fascist. He made a show of consulting me, but he knows damn well that if I want to pass this section of my certificate, I have to do what he says.

Well, I'm damned if I'm going to let an old fool stand between me and my diploma. So, it's game on.

Joint Thought Channel 1 Feb 2210, 09:00

Inspector of Wrecks
Remember that I've rigged up that special bailout route via the eye-movement sensor, so that it's faster than before.

Apprentice
Got it.

Inspector of Wrecks
When we go in, you grab Gwydion and I'll stick to Gilfaethwy. I'm sure that this visit we'll find the Mastermind entrance, so that we can see who's controlling the whole story. All right?

Apprentice
Let's get on with it.

Inspector of Wrecks
Oh, she's gone. Wait for me!

Apprentice
Hurry up! This looks quite straightforward. Gwydion and

Gilfaethwy standing in front of King Math. No sign of any women. I'm taking the Gwydion part... now!

Inspector of Wrecks
Yes, looks like payback time for the rape. Odd, Math's standing on the ground this time. He must be at war.

Apprentice
If you'd taken your character faster, you'd know that Gwydion and Gilfaethwy started a war in order to separate Math from his footholder. People have been killed so that Gilfaethwy could have his way with Goewin. He's not a bit sorry, though. Just like a Mastermind. I bet it's him.

Inspector of Wrecks
Right, I'm there. As Gilfaethwy. He's feeling pretty smug and is just interested to see what's going to happen next.

Apprentice
What about Goewin? I bet she's just been tossed aside like an old sock. Typical sexist space games.

Inspector of Wrecks
Now, now. Let me see. Math's decided to marry her to make good the dishonour she's experienced at the hands

of – at our hands, I should say. We're his nephews, so he's responsible for our behaviour. What I didn't realise about Math before is that he's a wizard as well.

Apprentice
I didn't quite catch what he just said, did you? But I don't like the way he's raising that stick.

Inspector of Wrecks
That's not a stick, it's his magic wand. I think that's bad news for us. Duck!

Apprentice
What happened?

Inspector of Wrecks
He's gone. Where are we now? The programme's still creasing I think. This doesn't make sense.

Apprentice
It's so quiet. We're in an oak forest. I feel quite different.

Inspector of Wrecks
Oh my God, this is beyond weird.

Apprentice
I can smell fear on you, adrenalin – it's sour.

Inspector of Wrecks
The smells are very strong here. They're about a hundred times more vivid than usual.

Apprentice
Yes, it's almost like seeing the path of a spoor. I can sense where a rabbit's paws have left damp marks on that rock over there. His scent's a delicious cloud.

You smell quite musky. This is like being a child again, and being able to pick up salt on the skin of adults.

Inspector of Wrecks
I feel jumpy though. I'm sure there's a threat here, even though it looks peaceful. I'm on a hair-trigger. Get ready to run. Do you feel it?

Apprentice
No, no, I'm sure everything's fine. I'm keeping a watch. That water has cinquefoil and liquorish in it. Let's get a drink.

Inspector of Wrecks
Are you sure it's safe?

Apprentice
Come on, you sissy. Call yourself a man? Look, I'll show you. See? It's perfectly secure. The water's… oh shit!

Inspector of Wrecks
See, I told you, I told you. Get ready to run!

Apprentice
What's this on my head? I hit it on the stones. Campion! I can't find my hands to feel what I am. I seem to have hooves. Campion, come here!

Inspector of Wrecks
You're secreting so much adrenalin that you're making me panic. There's danger, danger all around. Don't know where to look, where to flee.

Apprentice
Look in the water… I can't touch my head because I'm a stag. I've got a branch of horns on my head, like a candelabra. Head up, scent the air and that tells me every-thing I need to know. Yes, Gilfaethwy beside me smelling

of musk and hormones, my hind.

Inspector of Wrecks
This is confusing. Nona's playing a man who's been turned into a stag. That must be what Math was doing with his staff, he's turned the two brothers into deer as punishment for the rape.

Apprentice
He's done more than that.

Inspector of Wrecks
What kind of punishment is this? Two brothers get to hang out in the woods for a year, enjoying each other's company.

Apprentice
You don't get it, do you?

Deep breath, satisfaction. Pine needles, sour-sweet smell of doe.

Inspector of Wrecks
The forest looks fertile and how hard can it be to spend a year grazing? As penances go, this isn't so bad.

Apprentice
Long months since I shed my velvet…

He's turned us into animals because we behaved like beasts. But the point is that he's transformed Gwydion into a stag and Gilfaethwy into a hind.

Inspector of Wrecks
So I'm the female?

Apprentice
Flex my strong neck. Bow down, look upwards and I can see the tines of my horns: bay, trey, sur-royal and crown. Tilt forward and stretch my powerful back legs.

Come here. Let me sniff the piss spilt down the fur of your hock. Hmm. Aromatic, sweet with an abrasive edge. It's exciting.

Inspector of Wrecks
Your scent's disturbing. Testosterone, crushed acorns. Don't stand so close.

Apprentice
I need to smell…

Inspector of Wrecks
Geddoff me! You're acting like a stag in rut.

Apprentice
That's what I am! You're a doe in oestrus. Math clearly intends us to mate!

Inspector of Wrecks
You're making me nervous. Back off!

Apprentice
Close her on the oak tree, stop her from turning her haunches away... rub-urine... her tarsal gland tells me she's ready...

Inspector of Wrecks
Shit, you're my brother. Don't you dare.

Apprentice
No, I'm a dominant buck. Can't you see how my neck is swollen? That's better, you're getting into your part.

Inspector of Wrecks
Why am I squatting? My rear has a will of its own and I'm half sitting down. My body's insisting.

Never imagined that I could be two. Gilfaethwy and doe. No, three, I'm Campion, rapist and submissive doe all at the same time. How the body responds with joy to the rutting, spirit extends...

To have sex with my brother! With my assistant! To know the sound of her grunting behind me. That bastard Math.

Apprentice
Forget about weirdness. This feels so right. I'm swimming a stream which goes through her back, into her body and I feel inside...

Inspector of Wrecks
Mind of a man in a stinking animal...

Apprentice
Mind of the body, as the lichen lays in the moss and the tree sucks sweet water up, like a tide...

Inspector of Wrecks
Passive, like soil, no will of my own...

Apprentice
Till it explodes. And I'm falling, light-liquid, falling back

down from a red doe's haunches.

Inspector of Wrecks
Oh, the shame.

Apprentice
To be complete as an animal, nothing is better. To smell of come.

Inspector of Wrecks
With my brother!

Apprentice
What have I done?

★

Synapse Log 2 Feb 2210, 11:00

Apprentice
Campion hasn't met my eye since our last turn in the VR. It's not as if I raped him. It was all perfectly natural. That'll teach him to take what I experienced lightly. I feel like telling him that it's only VR, but I don't quite dare.

For me, it was a really interesting experience, a

chance to see what it's like to be a wild animal. I'm quite looking forward to the next visit. He's given us a day off, shut himself up in the lab, pretending to do dust analysis. But I bet he's just recovering from the shock of being a doe and being fucked by me. No, by a buck. Or should I say his brother Gwydion?

I want to say sorry, but how do you apologise for being a stag in rut?

Inspector of Wrecks

There's far more vegetable matter here than you'd expect in the atmospherics of a ship, even an Earth one. Of course, they had the usual hydroponics system to keep the atmosphere sweet and to give the crew fresh food. But those early systems were highly risky. Like keeping a fire alive by making sure it never went out. If for any reason you had a disease which killed all your plants at the same time and you weren't able to save a seed, then you were in big trouble.

She

I liked being a stag. OK, there was the hunger and

the constant nerves but I felt fit as a flea and I loved the forest. All those smells!

He

Now that we have those vegetable stem cells, we can grow anything from scratch, without having to propagate.

I know I shouldn't object to what happened in the VR, but I can't help feeling that the story's making it hard to be professional. I mean, how can you supervise someone you've mated with and whose child you've borne against your will?

She

Poor Campion, I thought he was going to have a fit when he realised that he was pregnant.

He

I'm an experienced enough traveller to know that you lose all dignity on a space trip. But that's usually to do with toilet matters, not being banished to a forest with your student, turned into an animal and forced to reproduce.

Mind you, the birth was kind of interesting. I've

often wondered what it feels like to have a baby. Though I guess that bearing a fawn doesn't quite count. Animals are better at it than women; they seem to suffer less pain. Even that was enough. But I never even lay down, just stood. And oh, the baby's sweet aroma when he came out!

She

So Campion and I are parents! And when the year of being deer was over, we went back to Math and showed him the fawn.

He

What's amazing, though, in all this, is that the sensations of being a mother were so much more sophisticated than they should be, given the primitive VR equipment we were wearing. I can't understand it. How did I know to lick the fawn's faeces and urine in order to hide his scent? It's as if instinct was wired into the game in a way I can't explain.

She

And Math seemed pleased and touched the fawn. And suddenly there he was, a lovely strong boy, much larger than he should be for his age. Though I suppose, I'd been counting in deer, not human, time.

He

I was horrified when Math turned the boy into a human child. That made it real, somehow. While we were in the forest, we were just animals. I was glad when Math sent the boy away to be baptised and fostered.

I wanted nothing to do with the creature.

6

Breeding Season

Apprentice
I still don't think it's fair that I've got to be Gilfaethwy this time. You said you'd keep me from being sexually molested again. I don't want to be the female like you were last time.

Inspector of Wrecks
As far as sex goes, we're quits. You've been raped, I've been topped by a buck. Look, we don't know what will happen next. You've just as good a chance of being safe in Gilfaethwy as anybody else.

Apprentice
Like hell.

Inspector of Wrecks

What was that? If I thought you were being insubordinate, you'd be back on Mars in a trice.

Apprentice

No, no, I wasn't. Please don't send me back.

Inspector of Wrecks

There are lots of people who would give their right arm for this opportunity…

Apprentice

OK, OK. I'll take Gilfaethwy, even if it means being punished some more.

Inspector of Wrecks

It's got nothing to do with what happened last time. I need to be Gwydion because it's looking more and more likely that he's the Mastermind. And if we can find his domain, then there's a chance that its archaeology will show us what happened on board this ship. After all, we have nothing else to go on.

Apprentice
Right.

Inspector of Wrecks
Now I don't want to waste any more precious VR time arguing. There's a limit to how long we can spend in this mode. Are you ready?

Apprentice
I am. Let's go.

Inspector of Wrecks
Oh, the forest again. Looks just like before. Except taller. And the smells, if anything, are even stronger.

Apprentice
It's not that the trees have grown, it's that we're shorter. Look!

Inspector of Wrecks
So we are. We're back to being animals.

Apprentice
Looking at you, I'd say we were some species of wild boar.

Inspector of Wrecks
Doesn't the soil smell sexy? I can't keep my snout out of the humus…

Apprentice
I don't want to be the bearer of bad news…

Inspector of Wrecks
Can you smell that fungus? Quick, I'm sure there are truffles under this oak. Dig!

Apprentice
But it seems to me that I'm the taller of us two…

Inspector of Wrecks
You're obviously not as sensitive to scent as I am, I'm a champion hunter. Here! Look! I've found the delicacy, which I snuffle, scoff.

Apprentice
Math has swapped our roles around this year. Gwydion, who was the male last time is now the sow. And Gil-faethwy's taking his turn as a male, so that both brothers get to learn what it is to bear young. Oh, that's funny.

Inspector of Wrecks
What are you saying?

Apprentice
*Because you swapped roles, you get to be the female again.
And you know what happened last time. We're meant to
breed! You get to bear the young! That'll teach you to cheat!*

Inspector of Wrecks
If I were you, I'd change your tone of voice.

Apprentice
Sorry.

Inspector of Wrecks
*Of course, it's perfectly fine with me to be female again. I
suppose the idea is that I bear another child. Well, Math
will dispose of it as he did the other. Can't even remember
its name. Hyddwn or something. Never see it again, I hope.*

Apprentice
*That's a bit heartless, even for a sow. To bring a child into
the world and then abandon it gladly.*

Inspector of Wrecks
I never wanted it, so why should I care?

Apprentice
Because, even if it is a fawn, it's our flesh and blood and we created him.

Inspector of Wrecks
I think you're forgetting that this is a computer game.

Apprentice
Even in a game, some things are sacred.

Inspector of Wrecks
Hark at you! Body of a boar, mind of a woman!

Apprentice
But if it's like last time, Math will turn our animal offspring into a human child. Doesn't that mean anything to you? I'm sure it's important. After all, we're in here not to play but to find out what happened on board this ship. Working out the values of the crew from the VR has got to be part of the job.

Inspector of Wrecks
At this point, I'm thinking it's just a game, with these ridiculous forays into animal nature. We're not even close to the part of the programme I want to find.

Apprentice

But surely this section contains relevant information. The crew was human, so it must signify something that the animal young are turned into boys.

Inspector of Wrecks

I think you're mistaking pseudo-medieval fancifulness for actual data. This is all decorative.

Apprentice

But it feels so much more real than it needs to be. Why would they waste resources on something that doesn't mean anything?

Take how we feel in here, it's breathtaking. I'm finding the forest floor so delightful that it's arousing. The excitement reaches around my bowels, and I shit where I stand, with the thrill of just being here.

Have you got over your snit at being the sow?

Inspector of Wrecks

I'll ignore that remark. What's really shocking is how easy it is to revert to being animal.

Apprentice

Those early VRs usually made people into more evolved beings than they actually were. This one goes backwards, down the evolutionary scale. It's actually much more interesting.

Inspector of Wrecks

It has its pleasures. Even otter scat tells me a story.

Apprentice

Except that our offspring will be turned into a human child, remember. It's as if we're beginning to generate a story quite independent of what we're experiencing now.

Inspector of Wrecks

That's the imagination for you. Look at the detail! I must say, you have a particularly fine set of nape bristles. Quite handsome.

Apprentice

Thanks. You don't look bad yourself, I love the little wiggly tail.

Inspector of Wrecks

Here's a particularly fragrant patch of mud. Care to roll with me?

Apprentice
What about our mission? This is too much like fun.

Inspector of Wrecks
I don't see anything else to do but go with the flow at this point. Got any better ideas?

Apprentice
What's that noise?

Inspector of Wrecks
I can smell humans. They know where we are.

Apprentice
Oh, no, dogs! It's a hunt!

Follow me! I know where the underbrush is thick and they can't follow. That's the joy of having such short, powerful legs, we can run to the undergrowth and use brambles and nettles as cover.

Inspector of Wrecks
We've got to survive this, or we'll never get out of the forest!

Apprentice
Don't worry, humans are no match for wild pigs, especially

ones which have human minds. Remember, if all else is lost and you're cornered, wild boars have been known to charge and attack their pursuers.

Inspector of Wrecks
I'll see you back at the mud patch in half an hour, when we've lost the hunters.

Tally ho!

★

Synapse Log 3 Feb 2210, 23:45

Inspector of Wrecks
Hychddwn, Hychddwn. Can't get the name out of my head, or how the little boy went so obediently with Math. He left us without one look backwards. I felt quite hurt, given that... oh well, never mind. After all, it's just VR, isn't it?

Nona's turned out to have a natural ability in the game. It's much more old-fashioned than the stuff the kids are playing these days, but she's got the knack of standing a little aside from what she's experiencing. I must say I'm beginning to rate her comments. Though she's cheeky and I can't have that. But what's the use of caring about discipline? I'm through. She won't be working with me but in the new unit. Still, it's important not to let standards slip, even now.

I might give her more scope in the VR as we go on. She's perceptive. And it's good to have another pair of eyes on the interior landscape of the ship. It's been a long time since I worked closely with somebody else. I'm beginning to like it.

Are you lonely, you old fool?

Reason I chose this job was so that I wouldn't have to manage other people. So that I could follow my own train of thought without interference.

So what am I facing now when I retire? A solitary cell. As much of my own company as I want. To come back home and know that everything will be in exactly the place my own hand left it. Doesn't sound quite so good as it used to. Still, I worked hard all my life to make things that way. I chose it.

Stupid, I'm feeling a little low. Must be the effect of seeing that kid going off with Math. Think I'll look out of the porthole for a while. That always cheers me up, puts things in the right perspective.

No, I won't look down on Mars but out into space. I like the way they put a telescope at each of the windows on this ship. It lets you view the skies at any wavelength you choose, so that you can see the full range of what's out there. My favourite is the infrared. There, that's adjusted. No, I'm not interested in the black but in the dense areas of stars, the parts of the sky so speckled with light that it looks like an inflamed rash, as if the whole universe were in a fever.

Oh, and look over there. Filigree gas and clouds from a nebula, dense as the petals of a rose. With shock waves reaching far into the pulsing sky.

7

The Wild

Joint Thought Channel 4 Feb 2210, 09:00

Inspector of Wrecks
Here we go again. Another day, another forest.

Apprentice
No, same forest, different animals.

Inspector of Wrecks
What are we this time?

Apprentice
Wolves. It was good of you to take the female role again.

Inspector of Wrecks
Not at all, my pleasure. After last time as a sow, I've come to enjoy bearing children. I love that feeling of a new life stirring inside me. It was quite a wrench to see the piglet

being changed into a human child and taken away by Math.

Apprentice
Yes, he was handsome, wasn't he? What was he called again?

Inspector of Wrecks
Typical male, can't remember the name of your own off-spring!

Apprentice
They all sound so alike.

Inspector of Wrecks
The first was Hyddwn. The piglet was Hychddwn. I wish they could stay with us, so that we could see how they grow.

Apprentice
You've changed your tune. Is that Campion speaking or Gilfaethwy?

Inspector of Wrecks
Campion. Gilfaethwy couldn't give a shit. He just wants to get the punishment over as quickly as possible. No, seriously, it worries me about the boys.

Apprentice

Well, Math could hardly leave them with two brothers who are still busy living as animals in the forest, and different species from the offspring. And two who don't care about anything other than getting their own way. Hardly parent material.

Inspector of Wrecks

No, I suppose not. But I wonder what will become of them? If this year is anything like the other two, then there will be another little one. Three in all.

I don't know how effective this punishment has been. Fascinating for us. You're Gwydion this time. What have you learned?

Apprentice

Hard to say. He doesn't give a thought to the children once they're in Math's hands. There's a terrible hard streak in Gwydion. If you're in his world, nothing's too much trouble. If you're outside, he won't lift a finger.

Inspector of Wrecks

What else do you notice?

Apprentice
What I don't understand about Gwydion is why he thought for a second that Math wouldn't catch him and Gilfaethwy. Goewin was bound to tell the king what had happened to her when he got back from war.

Inspector of Wrecks
Perhaps he's like one of those compulsive liars who seem to want to be caught?

Apprentice
There's something to that. But it's more. He's missing the moral element to his character. He's like a poet who sees everything in his work as a technical, rather than a human, problem.

Isn't it interesting how we're being turned into animals that are higher and higher up the food chain? What eats wolves? Not many creatures, whereas deer and boar are staple foods for forest dwellers. Not even humans hunt wolves for food.

Inspector of Wrecks
So what have we learned so far about the person who's programmed this world?

Apprentice

He's created a realm which is highly sophisticated, much more evolved than we might have expected.

Inspector of Wrecks

Yes, that is a puzzle. And we know that it's generative, that it creates stories beyond its own scope, with the children we've made here in the forest.

Apprentice

Who knows what kind of narrative those children could generate?

Inspector of Wrecks

Absolutely. There's something else I can't quite put my finger on, but which is much clearer in this third punishment. It's a world which is…

Apprentice

Dog eat dog? Or, rather, wolf eat pig? Do you mean predatory?

Inspector of Wrecks

It's not quite that, but it's close. It's something to do with how this programme treats the body.

Apprentice

That'd be the magic aspect of things. The way wizards take bodies and do what they want with them.

Inspector of Wrecks

Do you think the Mastermind is a wizard?

Apprentice

Well, yes, in a technical sense, in that he makes the rules of the game and we have to abide by them.

Inspector of Wrecks

But I still can't get those three missing crew members out of my mind. The two men and a woman.

Apprentice

Like the three absent children. Sorry, I don't know what made me say that. The third one, the wolf cub, isn't even born yet.

Inspector of Wrecks

I still believe that the story of what happened to the crew is locked in here. Might as well continue with our year of being wolves.

Apprentice

Yessir! I wouldn't have believed that it was possible to have a keener olfactory sense than a pig, but I'm getting news of fresh meat down near the river. Do you smell what I'm smelling?

Care to run with me for a while?

Inspector of Wrecks

I do. I think we're about to have a feast.

Apprentice

Come on, she-wolf. Hurry up and let's go! The crows are already there.

Inspector of Wrecks

Your eyes, with the dark circles around the light irises are terrifying.

Apprentice

Come on, slowcoach!

Inspector of Wrecks

Those eyes. For a moment, I saw something watching me through them. Something that has no concern at all for my welfare. It took a long, deep look, as if it were calmly trying to work me out.

Apprentice
Ah, there's the corpse!

Inspector of Wrecks
Before it destroys me.

The male wolf's faster than me and when I catch up, he's in a frenzy of eating. Hey! Leave some for me!

Apprentice
A fawn. I plunge in my jowls and wear the blood like light on my face.

★

Synapse Log 4 Feb 2210, 18:50

Apprentice

I'm beginning to like Campion. He's smarter than he looks. Though I don't know what he's on about half the time. Clever of him to take the female roles. He's been respectful. After that rape when I was Goewin, I don't think I could have been the passive one in all that incest and bestiality. He's not to know what happened to me on Mars surface. I've had to work hard to hide it in the Joint Thought Channel, but I'm pretty sure that he hasn't a clue. A repeat of that would destroy me. I told him I'd kill him if I was raped again in VR and I meant it.

We've done the magic three years in the forest; it should be the end of our punishment. Can't wait to see what the programme does next.

Right, I'm all in. Who'd have thought that following an entertainment system could be so exhausting? Channeller on. Good night.

8

Offspring

Joint Thought Channel 5 Feb 2210, 09:00

Inspector of Wrecks
This time, I'd like you to take the Gwydion role again, paying especial attention to the kind of magic he uses.

Apprentice
Strictly speaking, we need three people to go into the VR. Have you noticed how many triangles there are in the story? Gwydion, Gilfaethwy and Goewin.

Inspector of Wrecks
No to mention how many names beginning with G.

Apprentice
No kidding. Then there are the two brothers and their offspring. I bet we'll find more. Do you think these were the

roles the travellers created for themselves?

Inspector of Wrecks
It's perfectly possible.

Remember that Gwydion is a storyteller, and I want to see if it's his magic that's driving the plot. If it is, then he's the key and if we download his files then we're nearly there.

Apprentice
Why not download his files anyway?

Inspector of Wrecks
Because this is a logo-cryptographic programme. You can't have access to parts of the game in which you haven't participated. Simple device. Designed to keep the suspension of disbelief for the players.

Apprentice
Frustrating for us, because we have to live the whole damn thing. We haven't got many days left now before I have to report to Mars Surface. And we're no closer to finding out what happened.

Inspector of Wrecks
I'm very aware of time moving on. That's why it's important

*that we log as many hours as possible in the VR. Do you
think you can do longer than we did in the forest?*

Apprentice
*Don't worry about me. I'm up for anything that needs
doing.*

Inspector of Wrecks
*Good. So let's have a push today and see where that leaves
us. Ready to go in?*

Apprentice
Hang on, which part are you going to take?

Inspector of Wrecks
*Hard to tell till we see what's going on. I'll have to be quick
and decide once we see what comes after the punishment.
All right. Let's go.*

Apprentice
*Ah, back to the court. I've found and entered Gwydion,
next to Gilfaethwy, of course, and in front of Math. The
brothers are both back as humans. They seem to have made
up with Math. He's consulting them about who he should
pick as a new footholder. She has to be a virgin. I've said*

Aranrhod. New character. That might be the one for you.

Inspector of Wrecks
Who is she?

Apprentice
Their sister. See? Another threesome. Here she comes.

Inspector of Wrecks
You're right, I'll take her. Oh. She's a piece of work. Just like her brothers, who she hates.

Apprentice
Look out, Math has put his wand on the ground. It always makes me nervous when a magician's staff appears. This is a test for virginity.

Inspector of Wrecks
It appears that I have to step over it. There's something here between me and Gwydion, a secret. I hope it's not what I think it is.

Apprentice
And that would be?

Inspector of Wrecks
Incest.

Apprentice
Not again. This game is full of it. Gwydion and Gil-faethwy did it three times to our knowledge. Do you think that there was a pair of siblings in the crew? The two men, perhaps? Or a brother and sister? It would account for the recurring motif.

Inspector of Wrecks
Math asks Aranrhod directly, 'Are you a virgin?' And I reply, 'That is my belief.'

Apprentice
Slightly tricky answer. So, step over the wand.

Inspector of Wrecks
Here goes. But you know, I feel like I did in the forest. My womb… I'm sure…

Apprentice
Oh. That's done it. You've left a child behind.

Inspector of Wrecks
Nothing to do with me.

Apprentice
Come on! The evidence is there as plain as day. You gave birth to a beautiful boy. Listen, he's crying for his mother.

Inspector of Wrecks
How could he be mine? I'm a virgin. You should know. You were the one who recommended me. If Gwydion says I'm a virgin, then I am.

Apprentice
Come back for the boy! You can't just step over him and leave him, like embarrassing underwear shed in a public place. You've got to face up…

Inspector of Wrecks
I'll never forgive you. You've exposed me to shame.

Apprentice
Campion. Does she mean the public humiliation here, or something darker?

Inspector of Wrecks
Her mind is so angry that I can't quite tell.

Apprentice
What I'm saying is, do you think that Gwydion is the father of the child?

Inspector of Wrecks
You'd know the answer to that, as you're him.

Apprentice
He is, though he doesn't think he's done anything wrong.

Inspector of Wrecks
You wizards fuck anything you want!

This is typical old Earth morality. The women get shamed for exactly the same act as men, who face no consequences at all. Look! Math has picked up the boy and is cooing at him like a doting grandfather. He's clearly going to take care of him, as he did the three children we conceived in the forest. And Aranrhod's the one who carries the stigma.

Apprentice
Only because you tried to pretend you were a virgin.

Inspector of Wrecks
But this isn't real life, it's myth.

Apprentice
These are real children.

Inspector of Wrecks
Aranrhod only dropped one.

Apprentice
You were too busy striding out of the room with your nose in the air to see that you left another little something. I don't know why, but I picked it up before anyone saw it and hid it under my cloak. Look, you can see it wriggling.

Inspector of Wrecks
Did anyone else spot what you did?

Apprentice
No, they were too busy naming the boy Dylan. I suppose if Math names the child, he takes responsibility for it, that's how it works in these pseudo-medieval games.

Inspector of Wrecks
I'm puzzled about one thing. If, as you say, Gwydion

was the father of the child – not to mention the thing that you have under your cloak – he must have known that Aranrhod wasn't a virgin. So why did he try to tell Math that she was, when he knew she was bound to fail the test? See? Another instance of him being a compulsive liar, who secretly wants to be exposed!

Apprentice
He wasn't to know that Math would test Aranrhod.

Inspector of Wrecks
He might have guessed. Math's a magician and his life depends on the virginity of his footholder. Why would he risk dying for a white lie? He had to test her.

Apprentice
Math is our uncle.

Inspector of Wrecks
What difference does that make?

Apprentice
You've played female characters so often in here you're beginning to forget how to think like a male. Gwydion was trying to get one over on Math, to see if he could trick him.

Aranrhod would have enjoyed the status of being a virgin, knowing full well that she wasn't. Even worse, they would have killed Math, leaving the way clear…

Apprentice
For Gwydion to take over the kingdom. Nice family, this.

I've just had a terrible thought. Could it be that Math was the father of Aranrhod's child?

Inspector of Wrecks
No, that doesn't make sense. Why would he have tested me? He'd know for sure that I wasn't a virgin.

But what's he doing with all these boys he's adopting? What's become of them?

Apprentice
I can't find any information in my hinterland files about the three children from the forest. Do you have anything on Aranrhod's son?

Inspector of Wrecks
Yes. Despite herself, she knows what happened to the boy. He was named Dylan and as soon as he was baptised, he made for the sea. He took on the ocean's nature and swam

like a fish. Perhaps he was a seal of some kind. The ancient Celtic myths have selchies coming ashore and living as humans. Oh.

Later, the boy Dylan was killed.

Apprentice
By whom?

Inspector of Wrecks
By his uncle, Gofannon. Another name beginning with G. Another sinister uncle, a brother to Gwydion and Gil-faethwy.

Apprentice
What happened?

Inspector of Wrecks
The files don't say. Only that it was a great blow and most unfortunate.

I'm beginning to think that anybody who has anything to do with this lot is unlucky. The children don't seem to do too well. Look at Aranrhod. She wants nothing to do with her own child. And yet you uncles adopt boys but aren't able to look after them properly. We can't know how they are because they disappear from the story.

What happened to the three live children and the dead Dylan? Do they move on to play other characters? Or are they like real people outside VR, having stopped playing their parts?

Apprentice
Where do the dead souls go, if all the characters we see are roles? Aren't dead people just the same as those who, for whatever reason, leave the frame of the story? Are we their dead?

What does death mean in relation to this kind of VR?

Inspector of Wrecks
That, my dear, is a very good question.

★

Synapse Log 5 Feb 2210, 14:00

Apprentice
We're out for a short meal break. He wants to carry on as long as we can stand it today.

Something occurred to me. We're playing parts the dead people on this ship took often. Gives me the creeps, and yet it's a thrill to feel the shadow of an entity that's gone through the same gestures and emotions before. Like an orbit. It's strangely stimulating that we don't know at which point the part became fatal. Or perhaps I'm being absurd.

Right. He wants to go in again.

*

Joint Thought Channel 5 Feb 2210, 14:20

Inspector of Wrecks
Oh, look out. The focus is clearly moving to Gwydion now. You're leaving us. Can you keep me informed of what's going on while you're out of my sight?

Apprentice
I'll try. So something significant is about to happen. It's to do with the little something I picked up after Aranrhod stepped across Math's magic wand.

I go to Gwydion's room. It's gorgeous. All stained-glass windows and luxurious fabrics. Velvet bedspreads and solid oak furniture gleaming…

Inspector of Wrecks
Too much interior design. Get on with it.

Apprentice
I thought you said it was all significant; that no detail was too trivial to note. Gwydion's wrapped the thing in gold brocade and hidden it in the chest at the bottom of his bed.

Inspector of Wrecks
It's as if Aranrhod dropped a premature baby and Gwydion is putting it back in the womb. This is so interesting. I'll tell you my theory in a minute, if I'm right.

Apprentice
I'm in a different chrono-passage here, and time's flowing really quickly. Gwydion's forgotten all about the baby.

Inspector of Wrecks
Typical Gwydion.

Apprentice
Now I'm in bed, just waking up, thinking of something else. I can hear a strange noise, like a kitten mewling, coming from the chest. There it is again. Suddenly I remember the little creature I picked up. I open the lid.

Inspector of Wrecks
I think I'm right! Gwydion's acting like a surrogate mother, bringing the child to full term.

Apprentice
And there, instead of a squirming thing, is a boy, waving his arms at me and giggling. A lovely, sturdy, fully formed son!

Inspector of Wrecks
You see this a lot in late medieval mythology. The functions which previously belonged to the Goddess are taken over by men. Hence Gwydion's male pregnancy.

Apprentice
I don't see that matters in the least. What's important to Gwydion now is that he has this starving child who needs to be nourished. No use turning to Aranrhod, she's made it perfectly clear that she wants nothing to do with her offspring.

Inspector of Wrecks
But it does matter. These motifs are in the programme for a reason. Let me think this through. What we're seeing is the change from matrilineal inheritance to a patrilineal system.

Apprentice

Whatever. I can't think about that now, I have a practical problem. I may have a baby, but I don't have breasts.

Inspector of Wrecks

What the story's saying is that female creativity can be usurped by men. If mothers refuse to raise their children, or don't acknowledge their existence, then men are in charge of both politics and the domestic realm.

Apprentice

I'll find a woman in the village to suckle the boy.

Inspector of Wrecks

It makes me wonder about how the relations were between the three crew members. Two men and one woman. She would have to have been pretty canny not to be dominated by the men. I wonder if this is the trace of a power struggle between the three? One that might have destroyed them?

Apprentice

You've lost me now.

Inspector of Wrecks

But you've got to see how this is relevant, the whole ideology of the game. How can I say? It's the male fantasy of taking over all creativity, even that which rightly belongs to the female.

Apprentice
All I know is that Gwydion's devoted to the boy. For the first time he's willing to take care long term of one of his offspring.

Inspector of Wrecks
If the men take over all creativity, what is there left for the women to do?

Apprentice
In fact, I feel quite fierce about this boy. I'll do anything — anything — to make sure that he has what every child deserves.

I'm going to use my magic to its full extent to give him a life, to make him legitimate.

★

Synapse Log 5 Feb 2210, 23:45

Inspector of Wrecks
Of course! The audio cassette. I knew there was

something we'd forgotten to log. It's just possible that it's still working. I'll go there now.

Move softly so that I don't disturb Nona in her hammock. She needs her sleep. She worked hard today. No need to put on the light, I can feel my way from foothold to handhold, I know the dimensions of this module so well, it's as familiar to me as my own body. Though not the sight of another person sleeping. In the gloom I can see that her hair has worked its way loose from its band and spread out like a sea fan. Her hand twitches. In her netting she looks like a fish caught underwater.

Torch for the module. Close the hatch between the two vessels. Press tape in. Nothing. Or, rather, a background sound like something turning. So it's not quite dead. I know, needs to be rewound. Tape may be fragile. Come on, come on.

As I'm waiting I notice little patches of mould growing on the hull. Our breath condensing against the cold bulwarks as we spend time in the VR machines. I bet the crew had to wipe the walls down with anti-fungals. Not like us with the chemicals built into the ship's lining.

Right. Press Play. A woman's laughter. A male voice in the background mumbling something. She has a light voice, full of joy. Says – what is it? – yes, 'Come on Urien, don't be shy. You know us all.' Some applause then quiet, then a young voice – a child – begins to sing! Can't make out the words. What? Bugger, what's happening? Tape must have snapped. Rush to press Stop, but it's all unspooling.

God! They had a child on board. Nothing about him – it sounded like a boy – in the log. And the company sounded, from the applause, like far more than four. But even in the most primitive of Earth space vehicles, they could have got to Mars in nine months. They started out with three crew members. Even if the woman was heavily pregnant when she came on board (and there was no mention of that in the log, you'd expect it to be noted), they still took longer than nine months to get to Mars. What had they been doing? Did they stop somewhere along the way?

It's no good, I can't figure it. The timeline just

doesn't make sense. This case seemed so straight-forward at first, but the more I look at this little ship, the stranger it is. And the story in the VR. Why is it like that? With all the fluidity between categories of human and animal? Not unusual, of course, in early mythology, but it's very unexpected in a Technological Age vehicle. You'd expect it all to be about warfare and aliens.

I'd like to wake Nona to talk this through, but I can't, it's far too late. There's something fragile about that girl, even though she's so feisty. I thought she was going to hit me the other day when she thought she might be attacked again in the game. For God's sake, it's only VR. This generation's forgotten that there's real life outside the Virtual Field. They never have any cause, it seems, to leave it. Still, for a young one, she's pretty good value. I'm beginning to feel quite fatherly towards her. That's allowed. If I had her for a year I'm sure I could turn her into a half-decent Inspector, and that's saying something.

I'm watching her as she sleeps. She makes small movements, like the leaves of a plant responding to the tiniest variations in light and temperature. In her dreams, she's leaning towards a sun about whose nature I have no idea and no way of knowing.

Try to sleep, now. Settle down. Funny – the body never gets used to the lack of gravity. Lean against something and you push yourself away. My limbs get lonely without the feel of things pressing against me.

Restless. Every time I start to fall asleep, I hear that tiny, high-pitched voice, singing a song I don't know from a part of myself that I've completely forgotten. It shocks me awake every time, familiar and alien at the same time. And it makes me want to cry.

9

Name

Inspector of Wrecks
This looks quite different. Like one of those primitive wizard games.

Apprentice
I know. I've seen them in the Virtual Museum. You each have a series of gifts and talents that you can trade in order to make your way through a landscape.

Inspector of Wrecks
Gwydion again. Why don't I take his part this time, for the sake of variety?

Apprentice
Why not? Do you want me to be the boy by his side?

Inspector of Wrecks
*Let's wait for a second until we see what challenge presents
itself. I'm assuming that, in the old-fashioned way, we'll be
given a task to complete.*

Apprentice
*That must be the child that Gwydion has reared. He's
grown much taller. Aged about − what − eleven, from the
down on his lip?*

Inspector of Wrecks
*Difficult to tell. Remember, we go through puberty a lot
earlier than the old Earth inhabitants did. He could be anything from nine to fifteen. The boy's big, though. He's like
his half-brothers. Their years in the forest seemed to add up
to more human years than the actual time they'd spent
there, which was only one season, after all. This boy has the
shadow of another realm on his development.*

Apprentice
But surely he's got no animal in him.

Inspector of Wrecks
No, that's not the suggestion. From what I remember from

*Irish myth, physical size is a way of describing the heroic. Cú
Chulainn was huge and his physical prowess exceptional.*

Apprentice
Cú- who?

Inspector of Wrecks
Oh surely you've heard of him, the most famous…

Apprentice
*Yes, as it happens I have. A long time ago I played a lot of
a game called the Táin. Just winding you up.*

Inspector of Wrecks
*Here she comes, Aranrhod. Why don't you take her part?
The boy hasn't been on the scene long enough to have much
to teach us yet.*

Apprentice
All right. I'm in.

Inspector of Wrecks
*This'll be interesting. The first time we've seen the siblings away
from the court. Perhaps we'll learn some more of their secrets.*

Apprentice

Her world is dark. As if I've put on indigo lenses that cut out the sun and yet make everything much more focused. You wouldn't believe the detail I can see. The boy's complexion, the shadows in his suede jerkin, darts in his undershirt.

Inspector of Wrecks

She was a bit like that when I played her yesterday. But I don't remember the eyesight thing.

Apprentice

I feel she's been brooding, all on her own in her fortress and is ready to wage war against her brothers. At this point she has nothing to lose. She doesn't know who the young boy is, and asks Gwydion.

Inspector of Wrecks

Look how the décor reflects the nature of the interaction between the characters. That's very sophisticated for an early programme. We're on a beautiful chequered marble floor, like a chessboard. Perhaps we're about to play a power game. That's a lovely perspective effect, a visual logic. First move, Gwydion: 'This boy is a son of yours.'

Apprentice
*This part of the game is formal, courtly. Aranrhod replies,
'Alas man, what has come over you, putting me to shame,
and pursuing my shame by keeping him as long as this?'*

Inspector of Wrecks
*If I were a literary critic, I'd note the repetition of the word
shame here. And underline the gesture of covering up, both
in Aranrhod's words (what is shame's gesture but a covering
of the blushing face?) and in Gwydion's action in hiding the
little something in his clothes and in his chest until it grew
up into this boy.*

Apprentice
*You did tell me at the beginning not to be afraid of noting
my reactions, however subjective. Does that still hold?*

Inspector of Wrecks
*More than ever. You might as well, as we're no closer to
knowing what's going on.*

Apprentice
*Well this reminds me of being a very young child, with my
brother. You know, before you can really tell each other apart.*

Inspector of Wrecks

As if the characters weren't wholly differentiated from each other. That happens in the dreamlike early human myths and in this one. Think of it – men turn into animals, siblings are lovers, wild animals are princes. All the categories bleed.

Apprentice

I'm looking at Gwydion with a creative hatred, waiting for a chance to get back at him.

Inspector of Wrecks

More flowery language now, as if rage required elaborate courtesy from Gwydion: 'By my confession to God, you are a wicked woman. It is because of him you are angry, since you are no longer called a virgin. Never again will you be called a virgin.'

Apprentice

Infuriating man! I used to be his favourite, all those loving words in secret corners, the flattery I was stupid enough to believe and now I've lost everything. He trumped me in public.

This is Nona talking now, not Aranrhod. Isn't it just typical that Gwydion doesn't think at all about his role in this shame? He's only concerned about how things look on the surface.

Inspector of Wrecks
That's a magician for you. Impression is all in the confidence trick of illusion.

Apprentice
Well, as a mother I still have some power left. The power to withhold.

Inspector of Wrecks
You wouldn't dare.

Apprentice
I would. If you're not going to acknowledge your part in this, then I refuse to be mother. I'll go further, I'll be our son's worst enemy. Just watch me.
    'Gwydion. What is your boy's name?'

Inspector of Wrecks
'God knows. He has no name yet.'

Apprentice
'Well. I will swear a destiny that he shall not get a name

until he gets one from me.'

I condemn him to limbo. To be blotted out in the pixel dust. To be nothing.

Inspector of Wrecks
I wish you wouldn't do this.

Apprentice
To have no independent existence of your own, but to be a pawn in others' games. To have no face…

Inspector of Wrecks
Nona, I think this is violating the style of the game. The first bit was enough for Aranrhod's part.

Apprentice
So you take on the features of whoever is strongest beside you. May you never know your own mind, but be always swayed by the latest argument.

Inspector of Wrecks
Nona, calm down!

Apprentice
So you change with the wind and have no core. No solid

ground under you. May you hate yourself…

Inspector of Wrecks
Your heartbeat's gone crazy. Nona! You need to leave. Now, this minute.

Apprentice
You shall have no self.

Inspector of Wrecks
I'm using the Emergency Exit switch and taking you with me. One, two, now!

★

Synapse Log 6 Feb 2210, 09:45

Inspector of Wrecks
She's with me, crying. I hold her awkwardly in zero gravity. Pat her back. I've never seen a person exceed their role like that. The Mastermind of this programme didn't design a pre-set role to withstand that kind of internal boost. It was clearly dangerous to her. Breathing's shallow but she's calming down. Waving me away, telling me she's sorry and that she's fine.

I look dubious but she says she's OK and wants to go back. I say, take ten.

I've heard of hysteria like this before. I forgot she's not a qualified professional, because it seemed to come so easily to her. It takes years to learn where your weak spots are, not to let the scenarios trigger them. What a fool I was, I've pushed her too far…

★

Joint Thought Channel 6 Feb 2210, 10:00

Inspector of Wrecks
Are you sure you want to go back in? You don't have to.

Apprentice
I want to. I'm sorry. That won't happen again.

Inspector of Wrecks
I don't know if I should let you.

Apprentice
Oh please! Don't you see that my reaction might mean that we're getting somewhere? You said that everything was information. Well, let's just log it and move on.

Inspector of Wrecks
That's a pretty mature way of looking at your emotional life.

Apprentice
Look, I'm a grown-up and I want in. I can't go home without knowing what happened. I'd always wonder. Please let me carry on.

Inspector of Wrecks
I'm just as keen to work this out.

OK. I won't push you about what happened to you. I don't need the details or even the outline. But I do need to know if you get close to feeling like that again. So I'll let you back in on one condition. That you promise to bale out before you reach that point.

Apprentice
I promise. I can do it.

Inspector of Wrecks
Don't make me regret this, or make a mess of my last assignment before I retire. You could ruin my blameless record, my good name forever...

This time you take Gwydion and I'll be the dame. Again. I'm beginning to think you don't like playing women.

That's better, a smile. Take some glucose and a protein drink and we'll try again.

★

Joint Thought Channel 6 Feb 2210, 10:10

Inspector of Wrecks
Let me do the lion's share of this visit.

Apprentice
Fine.

Inspector of Wrecks
So I'm Aranrhod and I'm in my fort, brooding. I fancy this palace is made of dark glass. She looks out on the world with the clarity of rage.

I know that Gwydion's part of this scene, but he's nowhere in evidence. You stand back, and we'll take it from Aranrhod's point of view. I want you to keep your mind alert to notice if there's anything strange about the characters' relation to the child.

Apprentice
Do you have a special reason for that?

Inspector of Wrecks
I do. But I haven't got time to explain now. I discovered something last night that makes me think that kids are the key.

Apprentice
You look very beautiful, like the Wicked Stepmother in Snow White.

Inspector of Wrecks
You know that film? I am surprised. I suppose there's a Seven Dwarves *neuro game.*

Apprentice
You got it.

Inspector of Wrecks
I look out of the window at the sea. It sparkles, like my hatred. There are porpoises rolling in the bay. And a ship. A Spanish vessel by the look of her.

I watch her anchor in the lee and wonder what goods they have aboard. I'm hungry for figs, fine wines or satin for dresses.

Apprentice
You're getting really good at being a woman!

Inspector of Wrecks
Behave, or I'll make you be her again.

Apprentice
I'll be quiet.

Inspector of Wrecks
Not too quiet, I hope. I need a woman's eye on this to make sure I don't miss a nuance or fact to do with being female.

I have a telescope at the window and I train the lens on the caravel with her bright, trailing flags. Two men are working on deck. What are they doing? Are they making clothes? I ask the servants.

Shoemakers from Seville, they say.

Go out to see them, ask what they have that would interest a lady.

So out they row. I watch the Spaniards talking as, slowly, the ship turns with the tide. Back comes a servant, with a bundle of something clutched to his chest.

Cordovan leather, so finely cured it folds like silk. It's tooled with gold.

Apprentice
Any girl with sense would kill for a pair of handmade Spanish shoes. Put your bare foot on a piece of paper, trace the outline and send it to the shoemakers with your choice of texture and colour.

Inspector of Wrecks
Back to the telescope. I watch the pantomime of servants rowing out with the tide. Up on deck. Long conversation with the craftsmen, who set to work with great flourish.

Servants row back. Ah! My shoes.

Apprentice
They look very big, as if they were for a man. Try them on, but I'm certain.

Inspector of Wrecks
There's plenty of room…

Apprentice
Far too big. They should be snug here. And here. If you're paying for handmade shoes, I shouldn't be able to put my thumb in between your heel and the shoe.

Inspector of Wrecks
They do slip when I walk.

Apprentice
Send them back, no question. Make them do it again.

Inspector of Wrecks
You do learn some unexpected things on this job. OK, I do what you say. Servant comes back. The shoes had better be right this time, or else.

That's better. Bit of a struggle to put them on. They look good!

Apprentice
Come here. Let me look. Can you feel your big toe against the end of the shoe?

Inspector of Wrecks
Yes.

Apprentice
They're too small. These shoes will never keep their shape. Walk over to the wall. Are they comfortable?

Inspector of Wrecks
No. The heel's digging in at the back.

Apprentice
*Hopeless! These guys are amateurs. Only one thing to do.
Go out to the ship yourself.*

Inspector of Wrecks
*Come with me, will you? I need your opinion. Come on!
Before evening falls. Remind me, Nona, which part are you?*

Apprentice
*I thought I was Gwydion. But there's been nothing to do.
Might as well come along with you until I get the cue.*

Inspector of Wrecks
*Row, row, row out to the caravel. Take an imperious tone of
voice with the shoemakers. Tell them the shoes are all wrong.
Here, they can measure my feet. I'll wait while they work.*

*The old man's bowed over his work and the fair-headed
boy stands, restless beside him. The kid toys with a bow
and arrow.*

*I hear the trickle of the tide soothing under the hull. Late
afternoon sun, low in the sky, makes me drowsy. The breeze*

tugs the fine hairs at the nape of my neck.

Suddenly a tiny bird – a wren – lands on a stanchion.

Apprentice
Campion, look out, I've found my part.

Inspector of Wrecks
Be quiet or you'll startle the bird.

Apprentice
Campion, you need to know…

Inspector of Wrecks
Don't speak unless spoken to. I'm watching, entranced.

Apprentice
But…

Inspector of Wrecks
When, suddenly confident, no longer slouching, the boy stands up straight, like a man, and shoots an arrow which hits the wren not in its tiny torso but between the tendon and the bone of its leg.

    'Bravo! The blond has a skilful hand!'

Apprentice
I tried to warn you. Aranrhod, look round. Gwydion was disguised as the cobbler. You've given the boy his name.

Inspector of Wrecks
It's a trick.

Apprentice
I heard you call him Lleu Llaw Gyffes, which means Light has a Skilful Hand. The boy's been sanctioned by his mother.

Inspector of Wrecks
I'm sweating now. Light is the enemy in space. It's heat, corrosion, speed and age. I survive by shielding myself from light and now we've let it into the heart of the ship.

Apprentice
Campion, don't panic. It's only a name.

Inspector of Wrecks
No, it's not. It's the cumulative radiation that will kill me with cancer soon after I retire. Sometimes, the light's so bright I feel there's nothing I can't perceive. Then, from a slightly different angle, my helmet becomes opaque and I'm blind because I see nothing but myself.

★

Synapse Log 6 Feb 2210, 19:00

Apprentice

In a way, it's a relief to see that it wasn't just me who can freak in VR, that Campion's human. It's odd that the story's hit sore spots in both of us. I hope he doesn't note my panic in his report back to the Department. Now that it's happened to him too, I think it's less likely.

This part of the VR's more straightforward than the forest sections. Aranrhod issues her curse, Gwydion finds a way around it, curse avoided. It's obvious that there are going to be three tasks, as in all fairy tales. We already know the second. When Gwydion revealed himself and Lleu – got to get used to that strange name for the boy – Aranrhod spat out that the child would never get arms until she gave him weapons herself and this she swore she'd never do.

Inspector of Wrecks

If I didn't think I was being paranoid, I'd say that

Nona and I were being sussed out by the programme. What happened to me back there was strange. As if the name of the boy set off a note that vibrated deep inside me, waking some atavistic memories in me. A boy named Light…

She

He probably thinks that I was raped, and that's why I went apeshit. Well I was, but not physically. Don't want to say too much for the log. But you try being raised as a child without your own story, just an afterthought in somebody else's. The speeches all theirs and never yours. The choices always going one way, your view counting for nothing. How you learn to hide, not to show what you want so it can't be ignored. Till you no longer know what a person like you could possibly have desired in the first place.

Nothing like it for making you want to crawl into any story going, in order to lose yourself. You become addicted to narratives. Not your own, but other people's. He wasn't to know that I'm in recovery. For me VR is already dangerous ground. But who would have foreseen this? Six months of

131

technical logs and facts as a cure for having no borders at all to my self. I was expecting to read surges in circuits and biometric stats and draw my own conclusions. Instead of which I have to dig deep not to scream when I'm caught up in a work of art that doesn't have my welfare at heart, that needs my mind, but couldn't care less about the rest. Still, it feels familiar, which is why I'm good at the playing. Concentrate on the role that's required, whatever that is. But some parts can be dangerous to me. This one's worming its way under my skin and if today was anything to go by, Campion's feeling it as well.

He

Think, think what happened.

I was standing on the fake caravel's deck, lulled by the sea breeze and the glare reflected up from the water, watching the boy shoot at the wren. I felt that suddenly a beam was shone into me. It came from him, the way he reflected my own being back at me. But there was more, I was being scanned. Something was reaching inside my brain, searching and questing. For what, I don't know but it was being done by an entity much more complex than any of the characters in the game.

I'm tired. What started as a curiosity of a wreck is proving more difficult than I ever thought. Hell, I used to solve cases like this all the time, didn't find them so hard. I must be getting old. Probably no bad thing that I'm retiring. I haven't got what it takes any more.

It was like being snow blind. I used to think that meant that your pupils opened so wide you were dazzled. What happens is the opposite. They contract to pinpricks and never want to open again because the light outside is such a threat. So, at the very moment when you're staggering around, fully illuminated, your eyes are confined to their own private blackness.

What am I missing while I'm dark in the light?

10

Arms

Apprentice

Short day today. Did the second curse, the armour. As expected, straightforward.

He told me about the cassette tape last night. Campion thinks that it holds the key to the wreck. That the VR is an imaginative version of what happened to the crew. Long voyage. Boredom. Relations take on a dynamic of their own, unforeseen by the planners. Someone screwed someone they shouldn't have. Illicit relations. A child born, his mother not happy. Et cetera.

What's wrong is the time frame. What if, I asked, they came not from Earth but from another direction? What if they came from a planet so remote that it took a whole generation for them to travel here? That gives them plenty of time to conceive and bear children. Might that be why the VR's so obsessed with young ones of every kind – fawns, piglets, wolf cubs, boys?

Inspector of Wrecks
Of course, it's ridiculous. It can't possibly explain how an old-fashioned vessel, full of Earth culture, could come from somewhere else. It doesn't make sense. Only time-wise. The whole thing refuses to add up.

Second curse was straightforward. Aranrhod: no arms for the boy. So Gwydion and Lleu – I still have a hard time thinking that name – go away to ponder. I made Nona take the Gwydion part, as I wanted to try something without her noticing.

She
So Gwydion's a master of disguises, yes? So I change our appearance and present ourselves to Aranrhod's court as two poets. Not my idea of entertainment, but I suppose in those days they were desperate.

He

Aranrhod does the usual medieval thing and invites them in. That night, at the feast, Gwydion entertains her.

They have a good time, as they're a match for each other. For every story that Gwydion tells, Aranrhod knows another. And it gets very late and the drink is flowing. You know the kind of night. When the sugar in the booze keeps you up, more awake than you've been all day and life is funny and fits neatly into your stories. Then everything's suddenly unbearably sad, and a song is called for. Then more alcohol until even your drunkenness is in tatters, you could go on forever, except that your eyes... and when you lie down, the room whirls around you.

She

Except that I've only been pretending to drink, keeping pace with Aranrhod.

We go to bed, the lad and I, and then I get busy.

He

As Aranrhod, I'm lying there, having been sick, with

a terrible hangover. I hear a huge racket outside: alarms being sounded and an armed attack on the fort. I get up and, in the confusion, can't work out who's fighting us or why. But the only thing I think to do is to arm every man in the place. The servants have their own armoury and have already taken out pickaxes and lances. I remember the poets! They don't bear arms, so I must supply them.

She
Next thing we hear is an urgent knocking at our door. I open and there's a wild-eyed Aranrhod, gabbling about an enemy outside.

He
And just at that point, I decide to do my guerilla move. I'm playing Aranrhod but I make a freeze-frame and slip into the character of the boy to see what we're dealing with.

The clamour stops suddenly as if switched off at source. I enter the room of his mind. It's a blank, a whitewashed cube. Outside I hear birdsong. Four walls, a floor, no furniture. It's hardly human.

It looks familiar.

She

I'm holding the whole situation in my mind. The soldiers outside, the attack on the fort, our disguises as poets.

He

Quick breath, then out into the racket and I'm Aranrhod again. The old man says that he's willing to fight. We look out of the window and my heart sinks. There are so many ships that you can hardly see the water in the bay. I tell my women to bring two sets of arms. I'll take care of the young one.

So I make him stand still while I strap on greaves over his shinbones, then the sabaton, the gorget, the tasset, couter, pauldron, cuirass then habergeon. Then I give him his sword and, finally, hand him a shield. I step back to admire him and see myself reflected in the polished metal.

Behind me, I see the old man put down his weapons. He starts to laugh. I berate him and make as if to help dress him too. He asks me if the boy's properly armed. I say he is, that I did it myself.

Then I recognise them both: Gwydion and Lleu.

And it suddenly hits me. I've been tricked again. I rush to the window and the ships are gone.

She
I can't help liking it when Gwydion gets his way. Aranrhod was furious this time, beside herself at having been tricked twice.

He
I look at the boy and he appears… more substantial. What I'm watching is the birth of the child into the adult world.

She
Still, it was a terrible curse, her third. First she called Gwydion an evil man and then said, 'I will swear a destiny on the boy that he will never have a wife from the race that is on this earth at present.'

He
Lonely forever.

She
Gwydion will think of something straightforward to get round her words. I hope I play him when we

get to that. It's fun seeing the curses unravel as Gwydion walks the gaps between words and what they might mean.

He

That room. It's me. A boy who's been playing at being a man and has no life of his own to fall back on, other than what he gets by subterfuge. It's my room in the dome down on Mars.

★

Synapse Log 7 Feb 2210, 21:30

Inspector of Wrecks

This is ridiculous. I refuse to be spooked.

Nona's tired, gone to her bunk early and is fast asleep. Before we quit the game, we started on the next scene. That was a surprise. Instead of beginning to plot his trick, Gwydion went with Lleu to see King Math. I took Math's part and I'd completely forgotten that he was a magician. Or I never knew. Anyway, why would Gwydion go to him? Aren't his own powers strong enough to rise to the challenge of Aranrhod's latest curse?

One thing occurred to me. I've been thinking all along that Gwydion was the chosen persona of the Mastermind, but now I think that it might be Math behind the whole thing. We'll have to watch what he does very carefully on our next visit. This might change everything.

Nona was flagging, so I decided to call it a day. We left Gwydion and Math deep in conversation, as if they were plotting something. I sent Nona to bed.

Me, I can't settle. My mind is reeling with the reappearance of Math, what it means for the story. And there's been so much new information to absorb, that I need to go through it.

Nona sighs. She's dreaming.

So what do we know so far about this ship?

It appears to be a standard Earth vessel of the spaceship age. But its VR capability is much more sophisticated than you'd expect for that period.

I feel watched, appraised by an entity far more highly evolved than the game we're playing.

The paper log mentions a crew of three, two men

and a woman. And yet the cassette tape I found suggests that there were many more people on board. How do I know that the tape wasn't recorded on Earth before the crew left? I don't.

What if it was a record of a fleeting moment on board? What are the possible explanations? Stowaways. A log that lied. That extra people joined them from another vessel. And Nona's suggestion: that the journey they took was much further than from Earth. That's the most radical idea of all, a new frame that changes everything.

The VR may well be a more accurate record of the voyage than the log, even though it's through the eyes of the Mastermind. It's like trying to reconstruct how a person danced from a few heel prints left by shoes on a floor.

And why this feeling of being interrogated by the story itself? That could be myth. It's designed to describe the desires of the self as an archetype, so it's hardly surprising that certain parts of the tale, or certain characters should interest us more than others, they match our preoccupations. I've been obsessed with Gwydion, why is that?

If I'm honest, it's something to do with work. It's on my mind because I'm about to retire. I love the way he conjures a future for himself and the people he loves. That seems to be key – he's always using his magic to help someone else. His brother. His son.

What kind of magician works his magic on behalf of himself? A lonely man. A man like me.

Why did I give everything up for work? Because I believe it's good in itself. That every action of trying to see what happened is a blow struck for the real. That it's possible to know the exact sequence of events that led to disaster. That it's a service to others to be able to say: The mistake was in the calibration of the log, which error led the crew to ignore the blind spot on their port side which led to collision. That the chaos of which I'm so afraid is abated, for a moment, at least.

I love the sounds of the ship at night. The reactor's hum and crackling of the hull as debris hits us. The click, click, click of equipment as it digests its interior measurements, adjusting to light, temperature and yaw. The fans on the hydroponics, as the plants breathe and sigh to make us our oxygen.

I know we're in orbit, but it doesn't take much to imagine that I'm on the night watch of a very long voyage. I feel protective of Nona as she sleeps. She's the heart of the vessel for me. Someone who seems to need work just as much as I do. I haven't asked why, nor has she told me. We have a pact of discretion but for the first time, I have a student whose appetite for what happened is just as strong as mine. If I'd been assigned her earlier we might have...

What was it like for those people on a long-distance flight of years? In a closed-loop system? So that nothing new could come in or go out of their vessel? So that they had to survive only on the resources they had? How would you keep the sense of a day just by counting the hours? Would you be able to sleep without the cues of light and sunset? Wouldn't your fellow crew members' habits become distinctly annoying? How one slurps his food? How the other farts? As you got further and further away from home, would the same things continue to be important to you? The chain of command? The original mission? Might you not start feeling ill if you imagined that the ship was toxic in some way? That pollutants had entered the system and were starting to kill you slowly, that the very air you breathed was compromised?

And what about mutiny? Disputes on a spaceship can easily become a matter of life and death.

Campion, you're daydreaming. Get a grip.

11

Flower

Inspector of Wrecks

Nona seems drowsy today. The result of oversleep, perhaps. I can hardly get a word out of her before we prepare to go into VR. Not like her to be this subdued. Things had started to warm up nicely between us. Still, she's young. Who knows what's going through her mind.

She might have been sulking because I told her I wanted to take the Math part again, to continue to look for the Mastermind interface in his actions.

She's sullen when she agrees to take the Gwydion part. She normally likes him. I offered her Lleu but I caught an involuntary look of disgust come over her face. I could have made something of it, no doubt. An Inspector needs to do whatever's required to come up with an answer, there's no room for personal preference in this job. It's just unprofessional. When I think of some of the terrible places I've been. Space vessels tacky with alien flesh after fires or explosions. Holds full of shit where animal cargoes had been abandoned to die… Faeces so thick you could walk on it, like a carpet. No, you can't be fussy in this job. And this wreck is clean compared to many others, even if it's proving to be intractable.

I decided: what's the point of a confrontation about roles if not strictly necessary? Math for me, Gwydion for Nona.

Apprentice
Concentrate. Gwydion. At least I'm not Lleu. That whited sepulchre. What does that mean? When I think of him, I think of a room…

He
I must admit, I'm glad not to play Lleu myself. It's too painful to think of that empty space, even though

he has a name and arms. I, Campion, have a name and the tools of my trade.

Now, Lleu needs a wife. I wonder if Math and Gwydion could find a partner for me. That would be powerful magic indeed.

*

Joint Thought Channel 8 Feb 2210, 09:02

Inspector of Wrecks
Let's pick up where we left off yesterday. You ready?

Apprentice
I suppose.

Inspector of Wrecks
Right, here are Math and Gwydion. I think we missed this part of the conversation yesterday.

Apprentice
If you say so.

Inspector of Wrecks
It's obvious that some of the action takes place without us. Come on, girl! Be a little more alert, will you?

148

Apprentice
I'm complaining.

Inspector of Wrecks
Is that Gwydion or you?

Apprentice
Gwydion. I'm furious at Aranrhod. What kind of woman robs her own son of his rights?
 I will be his mother and father too.

Inspector of Wrecks
Math's sympathetic. He's used to taking in waifs and strays and wants everyone who is part of the family to have a place.

Apprentice
Does he mention the sons from the forest?

Inspector of Wrecks
No.

Apprentice
I know I'm Gwydion here, but I can't help but see things from Aranrhod's point of view. If what we think was right

and Lleu is Gwydion's child, then why should she stand by the offspring of incest?

Inspector of Wrecks
What are you saying? Can you blame the boy for how he was made? It's not his fault.

Apprentice
I suppose you're right. But I don't like him.

Inspector of Wrecks
Nona! Wake up! You're playing Gwydion. His father. You love the boy and will do anything to care for him. Keep in your character or this is a waste of time.

Apprentice
All right! All right!
I'm at a loss what to do, and need Math's help on this. Tricks with ships have been fine for securing a name and arms, but what's required here is a different order of magic. Math's clearly a more powerful magician than Gwydion, he was able to punish him.

Inspector of Wrecks
Aranrhod said what, exactly?

Apprentice
'I will swear a destiny on the boy that he will never have a wife from the race that is on this earth at present.'

Inspector of Wrecks
Think, think. What other nations do they have on the Earth? Animals in their various clans. You mated as an animal, Gwydion. How satisfactory a wife do you think you would have made?

Apprentice
As a she-wolf? Perfectly fine, if you want a partner who can kill and hunt. I'm not sure that's what's required here. The boy needs a wife who can hold her own at court. That person's not a sow nor a hind, I guarantee it.

Inspector of Wrecks
Let's approach the problem from another angle. What are the qualities we'd want in a wife? Beauty? Ability to reproduce?

Apprentice
To be faithful, and to be a companion to Lleu for the rest of his life, a comfort. To be a match. An answer.

Inspector of Wrecks
To be... a flower. Why don't we make a woman from flowers to be his wife? If we conjure her from this coming season's growth she's not of a race already on the Earth.

Apprentice
A woman from flowers?

Inspector of Wrecks
She'll be fruitful.

Apprentice
This must be a joke.

Inspector of Wrecks
No, Math's very serious. It will take the two of them, him and Gwydion, to achieve it.

Apprentice
And what about her?

Inspector of Wrecks
How do you mean?

Apprentice
Forced to be human, to follow a script dreamt up by two

perverts in order to please a bastard created by incest?

Inspector of Wrecks
*It would seem a good solution all round. An elegant magic.
I've never come across another tale with this motif in it.
Striking, I'd say. Very desirable.*

Apprentice
You make me sick!

Inspector of Wrecks
It's a stroke of genius.

Apprentice
I'll have nothing to do with it.

Inspector of Wrecks
Nona, you're breaking your part again. Gwydion…

*Nona, don't do that. It's dangerous for me and for you
to leave before we're finished. Nona! Come back!*

★

Synapse Log 8 Feb 2210, 10:10

Apprentice

So he says to me:'You can't storm out of the VR like that just because something in it offends you.'

And I go:'Oh no? Just watch me.'

'And besides,' he says,'it's just a story about wizards and flowers. I can't imagine what can be bothering you.'

'Then you're more stupid than you look,' I say.

'I beg your pardon?' he goes, looking ten times more dense and he sputters on, 'You can't try to control a story like that, it's going against everything we're trying to do.'

'Oh, is it? What are Math and Gwydion doing except forcing a plot to go their way? And you're no better.' That wiped the superior look off his face.

'What do you mean?' he goes.

'I know what you're trying to do with me. Mould me to be a little version of you. Because you're lonely.'

'But it's my job to teach you.'

'You're doing far more than that. You're hoping I'll make a Little You, to carry on your legacy.'

And by now he's going, 'But, but, but', like a fish out of water.

So I go on: 'If you think I can be pushed around by a saddo who's failed to make a life for himself and who can't cope with retiring, then you've got another thought coming. You're just a desiccated old fool and you're sucking me dry, draining the juice out of me!'

At that, he looked embarrassed and left me alone.

Inspector of Wrecks

In all my years in the Service, I've never been spoken to like that. The woman's neurotic. All my training tells me that I have to maintain an adult demeanour and not descend to her level of hysteria.

I think back to the scenario in VR, to see what might have sparked such an outburst, but I can't see it. Gwydion and Math are just finding their way around a curse in a most delightful and original way, I can't wait to see what happens next.

What can have got into her? Should I read the Riot Act? Or ignore the outburst?

It's not that I haven't got a private life. My work

life is it and when that's gone, what's left for me?

I told her to take an hour off and that I expected her to report to the VR suite at 11:30 to carry on. Won't do either of us any harm to cool down.

★

Synapse Log 8 Feb 2210, 11:40

Inspector of Wrecks

The girl's a No Show. I'm going to go on my own and finish the task in hand. I will not let the slip of a girl mess up my investigation, especially not my very last one.

Right, back to business. Here's Gwydion and Math in consultation together. I take the point of view of Math because I'm convinced that he has overall control of what's happening.

And suddenly I know the recipe for making a woman out of flowers.

Math says, 'Bring me oak flowers, meadowsweet and broom.'

Gwydion says, 'But none of those flowers are yet in bloom.'

Math: 'You're a wizard, make it happen.'

I watch as Gwydion shuts his eyes. And although it's winter, I notice buds appearing on the oak nearby. The whole tree is quivering as if with desire. Time goes haywire. Days strobe on the patient branches and leaves protrude, shrugging and sighing as the quick days pass. Then the catkins of male flowers descend. A jay leaves a branch and a cloud of pollen drifts to the next oak tree, where the subtle female flowers swell close to the branches, sticky and red. Gwydion brings branches of the fertile oak to Math's feet.

*

Synapse Log 8 Feb 2210, 12:03

Apprentice

You know when you're young and you have all day to look at things and dream? When grass is at eye level? And its seeds are your equal? How you make palaces from the sun as it filters through blades of grass and you can live in those mansions?

I wake exhausted from dreams of green. Creeping

bent, sweet vernal-grass, wood fescue, Timothy, great reedmace, wood millet. I remember how we would loop its stalk around the broad-leaved plantain and decapitate its dry, brown flower. I recall the acidic smell of skin having skidded along grass, the cold, damp ache of its smudge into flesh.

But I was brought up on Mars. I know we used to play under the biosphere on the artificial pastures there but I never knew the names of Earth grasses.

I try to wake up, but I find it hard. A caffeine shot will help, some food before the next shift. I feel like a loom on which something is being woven.

Wall barley, grass, pendulous sedge…

*

Synapse Log 8 Feb 2210, 12:14

Inspector of Wrecks
'That,' says Gwydion, 'was late May or June.'

Then Math asks for flowers of the broom.

'Why?' asks Gwydion.

'Because it's tough. The oak can self-pollinate but the broom blooms earlier, in late April, and its flowers appear before its leaves. Its seedpods explode in July when ripe. The medicines made from it are designed to purge, whereas the oak is astringent. And the country folk bring sprigs of broom to weddings as a gift.'

In the underbrush one leggy bush goes crazy and explodes in yellow, with a thick, rich smell of almond butter. Gwydion brings branches back to Math's feet.

★

Synapse Log 8 Feb 2210, 12:23

Apprentice
My chlorophyll dreams don't leave me, nor do the names of plants. Sweet William, stitchwort, wood anemone… It's as if there's a feed from someone else's mind into mine and I'm overhearing a world.

★

Synapse Log 8 Feb 2210, 12:39

Inspector of Wrecks
'And last,' says Math, 'the meadowsweet.'

'My favourite flower,' says Gwydion. 'Also known as queen of the meadows or bridewort. Most common of the fragrant weeds, whose blossoms are culled in the middle of July. It's good for fevers and a woman made from that scent – sickly but creamy – must be beautiful to look at. According to Gerard, the smell of the leaves "Makes the heart merry and delighteth the senses." Sounds like a winner to me.'

'We'll have most of the summer covered then,' says Math. 'Broom early in spring; a fragrant meadow-sweet July and high summer the oak with its flowers.'

So Gwydion stands there and pillages time to conjure up meadowsweet. And the tall stalks shake as if in ecstasy. They bloom.

*

Synapse Log 8 Feb 2210, 12:54

Apprentice

I stand erect. I have no eyes but a feel for gravity, from my dark, damp root up to the finest veins and the tips of my flowers. I'm a translator, a poet of the sun, transforming the spectrum into tiny hands that move in light's wake, stroking the world with blind but sensitive tendrils.

I have no ears, but my body bursts through the skin of buds, its surface area grows, and feels how vegetation scuffles, groans in competition for the light. I smell the stress that tearing, striving, being crushed, causes in wild garlic, dog's mercury and squill. And as the Earth turns, like a dancer with a pliant back, I shift my weight to stay upright in my perfect static pirouette until, with grace, I take my bow as darkness falls and close my leaves.

★

Synapse Log 8 Feb 2210, 13:06

Inspector of Wrecks
And then we join forces, Gwydion and I. We imagine the perfect woman for Lleu. She's sultry as early spring days, long, slender and bright as the stalks of Genista. She's modest as meadowsweet but has a whole spectrum of emotional life, as complex as its

fragrance. She's strong as oak, resilient as acorns that swell from the buds of the flowers. She pulls animals and birds in close to her, is a shelter.

And the body we conjure out of buds, flowers and seeds isn't an orphan. She's our daughter – mine and Math's. It's our minds that give birth to her, in the shape of our delights, our fondness, our grief. Maybe our failings. And we lay her to grow in the best of ourselves, making room for a consciousness not our own, but that of the forest's. And it feels like pain but isn't as we've woven her out of everything that we both know about love and awareness and we're sure it's enough, that its generosity can make up for the loss of a mother, that our meaning well will do right by Lleu and create a home which is a form of justice that the boy deserves.

And in the middle of this I, Campion, ask: What kind of being does a virtual world create? If two negatives make a positive, then can two virtuals make an actual? Have we just conjured up a person who's real? Or one who is death?

★

Synapse Log 8 Feb 2210, 14:30

Apprentice

I lie here with my eyes half open and something works its way with me.

I dream of cells illuminated by a soft green light. Chloroplast. Ribosomes. Organelles, packed tight like batteries. I find galleries of green within myself, strings of proteins, they breathe through fibres. I'm in a forest of amino acids – protein chains which sway, like saplings, then blossom with molecular flowers. I move like mercury through the maze of matter. Cells throb, growth happens in jumps. I stretch, luxurious in the light, knowing that my intelligence is a web of filaments and filigrees, specialised in feeding on the tiniest amounts for the greatest results. Inside is sap which is drawn out by capillary action and soon a new energy runs up my spine, a pulse of excitement. How will things look from this new point of view?

Everything's possible, ripens in me. I follow the sun and in the dark, I bow in obedience. I am unknowable to Math and Gwydion, hum with information that they just infer from their loud talk and posturing. I reach up to the spires of giant oaks and down into mosses where I gather myself in the heart of the root web. I flex my muscles with an old, old power.

Death doesn't alarm me. That makes me alien to them. I can make patterns from how things decay. I take joy in the humus and I bury light as easy as bask in it, so that the webs in between the fingers I stretch to their limit, and my ears and my toes are translucent and beautiful as decay.

★

Synapse Log 8 Feb 2210, 15:15

Inspector of Wrecks
I leave the VR, exhausted. We haven't yet seen the woman that Math and I've made from flowers. All in good time.

I get to the module and I'm knocked sideways by the smell. Nona's been shopping, quite brazenly, on the work computer and has bought, of all things, perfume.

She doesn't refer to the row we had earlier, but holds out her wrist for me to smell the fragrance she's chosen. It makes me feel sick.

Apprentice
Of course, I went for a chypre, as I'm a woman of mystery. Storax, labdanum and calamus – an oriental aroma since Roman times. Produced in France as Cyprus powder, with oak moss as its base. There used to be a fashion for tiny birds – oiselets de Chypre – moulded out of a perfume paste, requiring Benjamin, cloves, cinnamon, calamus and gum tragacanth as ingredients. They were hung in ornate cages.

I choose a dark fragrance. Floral or sweet doesn't suit my character any more. My skin must be changing, so I crave the aromatics that won't leave you alone, that you're not sure you like, but which your brain craves, like fermented food. It's the kind of perfume that's an acquired taste.

I tried quite a few, but came up with this modern chypre. Base note of oak moss, patchouli, clary sage, with flowery notes of jasmine and hint of bergamot, lemon.

Or there's this classic: Ma Griffe. In the base notes, storax and oak moss predominate, with hints of cinnamon, benzoin, labdanum and musk.

Or broom – Madame Rochas!

He

I don't know what to say to her. Such a cacophony of strong perfumes in a confined space could be construed as a form of assault.

I tell her, 'Get rid of it.'

She looks at me blankly.

She

I find it hard to understand what he's saying. I feel heat on my back, as the sun swings round. I leave him and his anger; move inside to my bunk so that I can stretch out in the light. I can feel it coming through the hull as if there were no ship around us.

He

Women go funny once a month. I'll give her this afternoon but if this continues tomorrow, I'll be going home early and dumping her. I don't care about the investigation or what they say. I can't have a subordinate behave in this way. Gwydion would never stand for it.

What did I just think?

12

Wife

Inspector of Wrecks

So she comes to me early and says: 'Sorry about yesterday. Won't happen again.' Everything's back to normal. Not a word about what happened. Call me a coward, but I let it rest. I'm just relieved that Nona's behaving like herself again.

Apprentice

And I tell him that I think that the game has moved from the VR suite and into my head. He says nothing for a little while then asks me, did I drink anything from the shipwrecked vessel's water supply?

He

My first thought was that she'd swallowed nano-bots,

a later form of VR. It was the intermediary technology between the ancient VR and neuro games, now
children have the transistor implants into their frontal
lobes when they get their jabs. But she says no.

She

I can try to control it. Do you ever hear sounds like
a roaring of waters inside your head, perhaps the
cerebrospinal fluids as they circulate round the dura
mater and the pia mater membranes? I've tried
listening to the noise, even as it drives me mad,
letting it roar to its full volume. Then, when I can't
bear it any longer, I hold it still. So with yesterday's
living dream. I saw it, I lived it and now I choose not
to let it spill out of the VR frame and into my life. I
can control it.

He

I pretend not to know what she means. But I do. So,
I'm brusque and businesslike. We put on the helmets
to see where we stand.

Joint Thought Channel 9 Feb 2210, 09:02

Inspector of Wrecks
The scene in front of us looks like a tarot card: The Lovers. Math stands between Lleu and his bride, whose back is to us.

Nona, if you like I'll take her part.

Apprentice
No, it's all right. You want to be Math for good reasons. I'll take her. It'll be all right.

Inspector of Wrecks
If you're sure. I just think that Math is king of this realm and that I haven't paid enough attention to his interface.

Apprentice
With what?

Inspector of Wrecks
That's the thing. I still need to find that out. So, you get to be bride.

Apprentice
And was there ever a bride like me? I'm the one who all

the girls are trying to be with their pinks and creams,
bouquets and manicures.

Inspector of Wrecks
And Math officiates and the two are wed. What's she like?

Apprentice
Full of awareness and rage to live.

Inspector of Wrecks
She looks all sweetness.

Apprentice
She isn't. She speaks in fragrances. Now her pores exude
the smell of almond. I wonder, how keen is Lleu's sense
of smell?

Inspector of Wrecks
Math's very sensitive. Not sure about Lleu. He seems
impassive, looking very pale.

Math's a kind of scientist of the forest. This is what he
perceives: top notes made from the sexual secretions of
flowers, odours mimicking the animal's own sex
pheromones. There's a faecal whiff there somewhere.

Middle notes: resins that also recall the sexual smells that attract creatures useful for pollination.

Top notes: floral. Innocuous, sweet. A cover for the real business below in the sex juices.

Apprentice
She's hypersensitive to light and has placed herself, like a fashion model, to best effect under the spotlight of available sun. It looks like vanity, but it's not. It's the drive to survive.

She dances without moving. Her mind makes large gestures in scent.

Inspector of Wrecks
I'm getting it, loud and clear. She's nervous but curious, puzzled by what's happened. There's stress in the mixture. A touch of toxin.

Apprentice
She stares at her husband. Her sight's acute but attuned to temperature. She senses the exact gradations of heat on his flesh, the scarlet groin and armpits, the way the body cools at its green extremities. To her he's a multicoloured body.

He turns to her and speaks. She can see his lips moving but can't hear noise, only as vibration. She turns to Math.

He vibrates at her too.

Inspector of Wrecks
Gwydion and I will have to work on that, she needs to learn language.

She
I'm a synaesthesiac. Noise runs through the filaments of nerves in this new… shape. I'm hungry and I need to eat light.

I look down at myself and feel a shock. What kind of a flower have I become?

The plant next to me takes my hand, his face grows larger. He smells disgusting and I pull away.

Then the full horror of what's happened to me hits me: I am a flower made of meat.

★

Synapse Log 9 Feb 2210, 16:00

Apprentice
Do you think the people who lived on this ship ever imagined that we'd be poking around, trying to find out what happened to them? If they had, surely they would have left more clues. An accurate log? An SOS

before they all died? A message in a bottle?

Maybe they did but we just don't recognise it. Campion thinks that it's all in the VR but I'm trying to tell him that it's moved outside.

It's as if we are the imagination of the ship. What happens between us is what it wills. Only he doesn't yet know it.

I feel autistic, as if the world is standing too close for comfort. Movement's disturbing, as I have to track even the tiniest change of angle, disposition. I feel light moving around me, and I follow it, inching like an invalid around the module. I find I like to sit where the sun hits the hull and I turn my face to the wall, basking. I've moved my hammock to the other end of the capsule, to maximise my time in the light.

Lack of gravity confuses me now as it never did when I first came on board. I feel I'm growing in a vacuum and my mind doesn't know which way is up.

When Campion talks to me, I look at his mouth, hoping that lipreading will make some sense of the words but it doesn't. So I nod, make sounds back, don't know what I'm saying half the time.

What's different is that I feel his heat wherever he is. When Campion moves above me along the cabin sole, the shadow he throws moves across me. After all, I'm married to light. I want the full glare of his attention, though Campion never gives it. I need it like food and yet the man is fiddling with logs and with manuals in which I've lost all interest.

I send out tendrils of scent which he ignores. I can hear what he thinks.

Synapse Log 9 Feb 2210, 16:00

Inspector of Wrecks
If I hadn't blocked my sense of smell after the incident with the perfume, I don't know where I'd be. It was easier than putting all the ship's air through a phero-filter, which would have taken hours and distracted us both from the task in hand. Time's running out.

She
My body still looks like itself, but I'm different. I feel phantom pain. I can't even locate it, but I know that

I used to be more diffuse, much less protected, as if this flesh which I wear like a set of rotting clothes cases me in.

He
This marriage of Lleu and the woman of flowers, I wonder if it can be read as a metaphor for what happened?

She
No, stupid, it's literal.

He
Funny. Where did that thought come from, out of the blue?

She
He'd have a fit if he knew that I hear him now.

He
So it's literal. An odd inspiration. I know that the human brain itself is a VR system, and that language is the second imaginative technology, at one remove from original awareness. By the time you get to VR – even the early systems like the one on board

the shipwreck – it all looks like a hall of mirrors in perception's funfair.

She
Funfair? Now you're really showing your age!

He
Funny, I could have sworn that tone of voice was... no, that's ridiculous.

Apprentice
I'll try an experiment. If I make the rootlets of my mind reach out into Campion's, how far can we go? I close my eyes, and try to make myself discern the areas of vibration, where the axons fire across the synapses. I send out tendrils as fine as the most delicate hair, up through his spinal column, round his tongue, hungry for the taste of his mind. I feed on his eyes and bump into the dome of his skull, so I feel his impressions.

He
Of course, being Protestant I believe that it's all a question of symbols.

She

I can taste his thoughts…

He

But what if…?

She

That's right, stupid. What if it's far more miraculous than that? If imagination isn't something that stands to one side, making a discreet version of the world but, instead, transforms the matter of every subject it touches?

He

Yes, like the Catholic wafer, transubstantiation!

She

Trans- what?

He

You mean you don't know the difference between that and consubstantiation?

She

Just joking. I do.

He

Nona? Is that you? How did you do that?

She

What?

He

I'm on Synapse Log but we can hear each other.

She

What do you expect? Now that we're married we can hear each other all the time.

He

What do you mean?

She

Now that I'm Blodeuwedd and you are Lleu.

★

Synapse Log 9 Feb 2210, 21:00

Apprentice

It's not as if I made a pass at him, or anything, I was just being consistent with the role he asked me to play. Supper tonight was as awkward as any we've had on board. But he knows that he can't ask me to be professional in this investigation and then complain when he gets more than he bargained for in VR.

Inspector of Wrecks
I'm at a loss what to think of developments this afternoon. I don't have a theory, find myself para-lysed, especially as now I don't know what Nona can hear or when I have my thoughts to myself.

She
As Gwydion would say, we're all storytellers here and so we can hardly be surprised when our versions dovetail or clash with those of other minds. The strange thing is that we no longer need to go into the VR for the story to be taking place in us.

He
The one thing I do know is that, after the wedding, Math gave Lleu a domain of his own for him to rule over. Good, fertile land. And what was it like? I have no idea.

She

Blodeuwedd stands next to Lleu and turns by tiny degrees towards her husband, like a plant that follows the sun till their mouths meet and, ravenous, she eats the light.

He thinks she looks gorgeous. She thinks he smells of offal.

He

I'm Old School and believe you should never anthropomorphise plants. They're entirely passive, don't have minds like us, they just react to stimuli.

She

Gwydion and Math's magic is primarily visual. They thought that a woman made from flowers would look good. But the body has a way of taking over the story.

Lleu is the light that, invisible himself, shows up all the other characters: Gwydion, who's determined to make a story for him, Blodeuwedd, who turns to him because she has to obey the sun.

He

If the VR story is, in some way, a symbolic commentary on what happened on board this ship,
then why the concept of mixing the DNA of plants
and humans? What evolutionary advantage could it
possibly confer on humans? Maybe that light is
plentiful in space, would be endless fuel if the ship…

No, that's ridiculous.

She

Campion thinks that he's so open-minded, but he's
only beginning to see it. That the ship didn't come
from Earth but from much further away. That it
came from a place so distant that humans and plants
had time to marry, like Blodeuwedd and Lleu, to
evolve together. What if we read the VR myth as a
literal, not metaphorical, account of what happened
on board?

He

Do you have any idea of the distances that kind of
evolution would require? It's madness to think it.

I have no idea what's going on. All I know is that

Lleu and Blodeuwedd cling to the ship that holds them, as if to the mother that neither of them has ever known.

★

Synapse Log 9 Feb 2210, 23:50

Apprentice

Even when I sleep, I'm not still for a moment. I tango with light and temperature. My mind counts its losses at night and thoughts, like vines, oscillate involuntarily in dreams. There are notions that my roots evade, like stones in the soil. I simply go round, seeking out moisture and a place to stand from which I can grow. I don't think, I revolve and break new ground and the burden I carry is heavy, as if I were lifting a boulder. Ah, the so-called sleep of leaves, far from inactive. I inherited habitual movements in order to seek just the right amount of illumination.

A plant is an animal that can't yet move. Except if it's in a spaceship. Using a vessel as her legs and a man as her servant.

Gwydion and Math's spells are all very well, but their cunning only gets them so far. They ride roughshod over people to get their way but they are absolutely no match for real, bodily imagination, for a plant intent on travel.

And don't tell me that a plant can't traverse vast distances, manipulating the desires of others to her own end. In that particular survival strategy, beauty is the killer.

*

He

Now that we can hear each other's thoughts, even if we're in separate rooms, I've given up on the Synapse Log and the Joint Thought Channel. It's enough to observe how the story unfolds.

Each day I wait until I hear the scrap of a voice, a clue. Then Nona and I – or should I say Blodeuwedd and Lleu? – start talking. And so what we are begins to take shape.

She

He's getting less formal. I notice that he spends much less time at his instruments. He needs me to be a dream of myself as Blodeuwedd.

I've no choice in the matter. I'm a prop in his story, never mind the rage inside me. I hide that and present the blank of my petal face. He has no sense of smell, so I weave a fury of fragrance in the air around him – a spite of galingale, used by Arabs to make horses fiery. He talks at me and I exude a cloud of musk for my voluptuousness that he'll never reach. He gabbles again and I reply with a mist of Japanese star anise, the mad herb, used to scent tombs.

Of course, they insist that I learn his talk. But does he ever bother to learn the language I speak incessantly to him?

He

I still think that the figure of Math might be our solution, an actual log of what happened on board this ship.

Lleu decides to visit his uncle at his home and leaves Blodeuwedd in the marital home. I think about missing kings and masculine power in the realm of magic.

She

If he'd smelt me, listened, he would never have gone.

The enemy of magic is time. They made me from summer flowers. Have you not seen the rust in meadowsweet blossoms, the brown of high summer as loveliness turns, as it must, towards its own decay? Have you not smelt its rank sweetness, like the stink of melon on the turn? Nearly delicious, but sickening.

He

Math the magician, the one who can make a home for the parentless, a kingdom for the rejected boy, cursed by his mother.

She

He knows that Nona's predisposed to drown in a role. So he throws her into a story in which a plant is kidnapped into the human realm to please two magicians, whose only concern is how things look. This she construes as a gross assault. I swore to kill him if I was raped again.

Let him go to Math and let my imagination change the terms of the story. He has no idea how sap burns in the veins of a woman.

★

She

What's the imagination of a flower? A bee.

I'm wandering outside the house one day and I hear a horn and dogs barking. A company of hunters. I follow and watch them, unseen.

The stag they're hunting is tired. It's been a long chase. This is no illusion with humans turned into deer. The animal's panting and I can see a crescent moon in the white of its eye as its pursuers close in from behind.

I gaze, entranced, as the kill is made. The process takes its course. Before working on the body, the hunter removes his outer garments and folds them carefully, so that they don't get soiled. He turns the felled deer on its back, spreading the hind legs. Then he makes an incision from the breastbone to the base of the tail. He slices through the hide, using the knife to keep the intestines away from the rest of the corpse. Then he severs the anus and draws that in to the body cavity, removing the intestines and bladder with great care and feeding them to the baying dogs.

The hunter's forearms are bloody up to the elbow. Here is a man not afraid of death. He thrives on it, feeds from the feast of real time.

Next he works on the diaphragm, cutting into the chest cavity and pulling out the lungs. He spreads that open with a stick, to help the carcass cool. Next he turns the stag on its stomach and lets the blood drain out.

Then he covers the whole with a clean cloth and washes his hands in the nearby stream.

Behind the tree trunk, from where I'm watching, I smell my arm. The same kind of meat, in need of dressing.

When he passes the house with his company, I send a servant to invite him in.

He

Math and Gwydion's magic works by distraction. It draws attention away from the undesirable aspects of life, inconvenient hatreds, like Aranrhod's rage against her brother and Lleu.

She

The hunter's a man who makes an art of death. That, I respect. He doesn't use conjuring tricks to get round language.

He made a ceremony of meat and I found that exciting.

It was only proper that I should invite him in.

He

But what happens when flesh and blood enter the VR? The story takes on a life of its own. A death of its own.

And whose bodies are behind the tale? I look, but I can't find Math or Gwydion, except in the layer of tricks. The narrative has entered an entirely new phase, in my body and Nona's and I feel that sight – realm of magicians – is now a liability. This chapter's written in blood, which has its own plots.

She

As does time. We sit at dinner and gaze at each other.

The hunter's unafraid of waiting and takes pleasure in letting things develop in front of him, without interference. I feel myself unfurl.

He smells me.

He

What if everything up to this point has been a distraction? A cover story to lead us away from what really happened here? And what if that was a battle between meat and magic? The body and imagination?

She

He's a man used to reading the air for clues of an animal. He kept the stag's scent glands, which he cut out carefully, to help him with hunting. He knows how to hide in the subtle forest of smells.

He

And what if Nona's being eaten alive by this myth? I need to get back to her, but Math and his talking keep me at court.

She

No need to delay, when things take place in their proper time.

He comes to me like an idea and in the darkness we know the same laws. I lean backwards and let the bees of kissing come to me, their parabolas making a fountain that falls back into a basin. My suitor claims the pollen of a nuptial embrace. Labellum, proboscis, bristle and saddle strain to get closer. He feels the silk of my skin, is not afraid to tear the folded pedicle up, it straightens like a spring. I'm rich as an orchid under him. My new lover's a guest at the nectary whose scent makes a conjugal tent above us.

And the shadow beneath us is Lleu's death.

★

She

He breathes me in. The following day I won't let him go.

He stalks me, the way a hunter should, every day a little closer. He pays me the compliment of hunting me blind, using only the senses of hearing and smell.

Second night, deeper, he feels me plunging down into the cold earth, seeking out moisture in the dark. Tendrils are a matter of principle, greeting the roots of trees like old friends, dancing with the molecules of birds decayed in the humus. I keep him with me another night.

Then he drinks me fully because he sees how flowers are meaningless in themselves apart from the seed and the falling leaf. The hunter loves me for how I was in bud and for my future descent into dead leaves and litter. And so we talk about how to kill Lleu.

★

He

With Math I learn nothing. At court, everything's going well for Math. He's there with his new wife, Goewin. He has a new footholder, a gorgeous young maid, whose lap he uses now that the war's over.

I'm none the wiser about this case, except that I'm beginning to suspect that I should rethink the timescales involved. Myth is a shorthand for what happens over many generations. What looks, in the story, like a surreal event is in fact a hugely significant change in a society's way of conducting itself. And in space, history means distance.

From exactly how far away did this ship originate? Forget for a moment how it appears – an Earth vessel of a certain age. Close your eyes to the design, the period touches, the tiny details which date a vessel. No, Campion, think, for once, with a mythical mind.

I scroll through the charts of stars I've memorised near to Earth. Corona Australis Nebula, five hundred years out, in the constellation Southern Crown. A smudged cirrus of debris and two bright eyes of new stars, where the radiation from explosions has cleared away the gas. It looks like an owl. Or the Pleiades, whose seven sisters are really a thousand or more. A blue light, Merope six hundred times more luminous than the sun.

I try to remember the next stage further out. As a boy, I took pleasure in devouring these sky maps but now I draw a blank.

I know. The dark nebulae are next, looking like

streamers in a background so thick with stars it's almost solid. Those are seen in the ionised light of stars six to eight hundred light years away, like Antares. Or the Helix Nebula, with its cometary knots, each one twice the size of our solar system, but looking like fancy stitches in a craftwork, or the firework of a second – a rocket shot into the night. Or the Snake Nebula, seen against stars twenty-five thousand light years away. Is that far enough?

She
Campion, I really think that, as Lleu, you should come home. That's our way forward.

He
Well, none of my other ideas have worked. You've taken every part requested of you, done everything I've asked. OK. Nona, anything you say.

★

He
Loving a woman made of flowers isn't easy.
 She seems compliant, smiles at my talk. She looks

as though she's concentrating hard, struggling to understand my words. I try to help her and explain the ways of the court, but it seems to me that she's bored. She goes walking constantly and I find her wandering outside the fort, as if she's more comfortable in the open air.

She

He thinks he's some kind of conservatory, a hothouse, in which I will thrive. He looks at me endlessly, I pretend not to notice.

He

I visit her timidly, like a humming-bird. I'm cautious, however, look at the bloom, dash off. I return, coming closer, lean back in the air, resting my wings on an invisible wire. Then I scare. Then finally I have the courage to sip. She lets me in.

She

Tell me, I say to him one day. How can you die?

I ask because I'm worried. What would become of me if anything happened to you?

He

So that's why she's always so distracted. My wife has been fretting. I can put her mind at ease.

She

And here's where the story goes all medieval again. He says it's not easy to kill him with a blow. The spear that would strike him has to be made only when people are at mass on Sunday.

He

Nor can I be killed indoors, nor outdoors. Nor on foot nor on horseback.

She

Tell me, I beg him, how exactly you may be killed.

He

It's a matter, I say, of acting out contradiction. I'd have to be under a sort of roof but out in a field. Then I'd have to be standing with one foot on the back of a goat, the other on the edge of a bath. If I were hit like that, I could die.

She
Darling, your secret is safe with me.

★

He
Nona? Are you there?

She
Mm… I'm half asleep.

He
So am I, but I'm thinking whose magic stipulations
are these? It must be a stage of the game with a
different series of parameters.

She
This tells me more about Lleu than anything before,
and I'm married to him.

He
Like what?

She
Well, look how he's already imagined his death in
such detail.

He

But it's a highly unlikely set of circumstances.

She

Lleu's a balancer. Look at his uncle Math, who's not to be touching the ground, but yet not in the air. Lleu could easily be knocked over.

He

Just as his life has been a balancing act between his mother's curses and his uncles' magic spells.

She

Exactly.

He

But this is nothing to do with Aranrhod's hostility to Lleu. Where did it come from? It feels like we've missed a crucial part of the story.

She

Yes, like maybe a bit where, as a wedding gift, Math decrees that Lleu will be immortal, except in circumstances which only he shall know and which should remain secret, or the gift is voided.

He

Then why tell Blodeuwedd?

She

Have you never told somebody something you shouldn't have? Something deeply personal? As part of a desperate bid for intimacy?

He

I can't say I have.

She

Are you quite sure about that? I can sense…

He

Quite sure. Lleu's life depends on keeping Math's gift to himself. Why would he risk everything?

She

Oh, I don't know. Maybe part of him wants to see what would happen if he stood in the riskiest place. Here's a man whose life has been subject to conditions. He can live, but he'll have no name. He has a name, but he'll have no weapons. He has arms, but he'll have no wife. At last he reaches full

199

maturity, has his own home, so no wonder he wants to live like any other man.

He

But he's not other men and he's inviting Blodeuwedd's betrayal. Why would he do that?

She

Imagine you're married and you love your wife. There's one thing you can't tell her. What more precious gift could you give her than that, a token that you totally trust her with your life?

He

But Nona, do you think he can trust Blodeuwedd?

She

That's not the issue, it's what Lleu must do to make himself feel most alive. He needs a betrayer. Think! He drew his first breath and was denied by his mother. That's the primal scene of his being. He loves his wife precisely because he's not sure that she'll keep his secret. It's the only language he knows approaching intimacy. Ironic, he gives Blodeuwedd

the secret of his own death and that's the most married they'll ever be.

He

Of course, his uncles have always saved Lleu's hide.

She

So far. But any man would want to prove that he
could make his way without being rescued time and
again by his elders.

He

What does Blodeuwedd desire most?

She

To eat the light and be free to follow her nature. And
what about Lleu?

He

He wants, I think, to be fully seen by Blodeuwedd,
apart from his uncles' conjuring tricks. His death is
the best gift he can give her.

She

I'm feeling tired. Need to go back to sleep.

He

I'll leave you alone.

She

Campion?

He

Yes.

She

You know you can trust me. Tell me your secret.

He

Bugger off. I'll tell you tomorrow.

★

He

Can't sleep. Keep thinking, going round and round this current scenario. Nona's right, Lleu's a balancer, he's always walked a tightrope. They say such artists shouldn't look down. But what if the thought of falling takes root in his mind? The air whistling around him becomes attractive and he wants to see the ground rushing up to kiss him with its real embrace.

After all, there can be safety in falling. What else is our orbit but a fall towards the surface of Mars at a consistent rate, so that we describe the arc of a circle?

Now I have to ask myself: What is my secret? I'm a man who's lived alone. But isn't the truth that I'd ditch the fortress I've built round myself in an instant if I knew that a person saw me, could imagine me whole, including my dying?

I know why Lleu's crazy about his wife. She's the only one who's bothered to ask him the basic question. How will he die? Everyone else is so deeply concerned with making him live. Only Blodeuwedd can see that his death is the sole event he has under his control. And he chooses to give it to her; he loves her for everything that will happen now.

This investigation has entered a completely new phase. It would frighten me if I thought too long about it, but it makes me so alive that I can't stop. This isn't professional, nor even sane. But I'm willing to wager my own death to find out what happens. Will she?

I look to see if Nona's sleeping. I catch the glint of an eye, but I might be wrong.

★

She

So I tell Lleu, You have to show me exactly how it could be done, so that we may avoid it.

In VR time it's a year later. The hunter's hidden in the woods, with the spear he forged each Sunday while people were at mass.

He

As Lleu, I'm enjoying the game, want to see how close I can come to the scenario of complete disaster without succumbing. After all, every time so far, I've survived.

She

I've had the arched roof made sturdy and thatched. And under it men have placed a tub, and filled it with water. Would you care to bathe?

He

I will, with pleasure.

She

So I watch Lleu wash. I admire him, how streams of diamonds fall from his body. I point out the billy goats grazing nearby. I invite him to see if he can stand on the tub and a goat. An experiment.

He

We laugh. Won't be easy. The goat is skittish and pulls against the halter that holds him. I put my bare foot on his warm back and it falls into a reverie. I'm balanced on the bathtub's ridge, not inside and yet I'm under a roof, standing tall between heaven and earth.

She

I turn to the woods and see a spear hurtling towards Lleu. It's a shaft made of time. No man, however enchanted, can stand against it.

He

It surprises me utterly. I jolt awake to find the emergency alarm sounding, lights flashing. The hull's been pierced by a javelin of light that hits me, stays in me, burns.

She

I find Campion in the docking module. He's jammed against a tear in the seal between our ship and the wreck. I close the hatch manually, cutting off the leak, then haul him back into our ship.

He's white as a sheet. Tenderly, I put him to rest in his sleeping net.

I wait.

★

He

Suddenly, I enter Lleu's mind completely.

I leave the scene of my death, an eagle.

13

The Tree

She

Think, think what to do.

Yes, of course, a Mayday to the Department, they'll send a relief vessel as soon as possible. But I need help now. Campion's absent or, rather, his mind's been taken by the VR. I'm in the virtual story too, so why don't I turn to one of the characters there for help? It is an emergency. Who would know what to do?

Not Blodeuwedd. She celebrates with the hunter, rejoices that she's free of her husband. Math? He's perplexed and saddened that all his plans have come to this. He's sitting in court, with his feet in the lap of a virgin. No good. Aranrhod? She couldn't care less.

Gwydion's the man. The one who'll never give up on Lleu. He's never discouraged and won't take no for an answer. His magic will take on even the most hostile of circumstances.

Because he trusts his imagination.

★

He

I feel overwhelming shame. For telling all. For being betrayed and killed by Blodeuwedd. I fly up from my body. I should have died, but someone has rescued me with a spell for which I never asked. Gwydion or Math intent, as ever, on making me live when I choose to die, so I flee.

I rise almost vertically, with no regard for the Earth now miles below me.

I soar till I can hardly breathe, into the fierce winds of the stratosphere, up to the dark of night, the stars.

★

She

Campion, I'm coming! With Gwydion's help.

I lie next to the old man in his net and hold him. I close my eyes, let Gwydion's cunning take possession of me. We've gone so deep into this game that, it seems, we can choose our roles at will. Or is it that they pick us? No matter. It's Gwydion I want, and Gwydion I get.

I see Campion and Lleu now as one mind. I search high and low for where he might be after that fatal blow. Am I looking for Campion or for Lleu?

★

He

I reach the zenith of my flight and hang there a moment in space. I'm perfectly balanced between two minds. Suddenly, I'm out in space, standing on nothing. I seem to float.

Campion looks down at the surface of Mars. Wind shadow streaks make craters look like comets. I take in Noctis Labyrinthus and the chasms bitten out of the rocks. Dust devils streak the rippled flats of Argyre Planitia. Phobos passes over the volcano Ceraunius Tholus.

Then I fall back into gravity. Lleu, the tumbler. A bird of prey, I stoop toward my end.

As Lleu I pick the most remote valley I can find on Earth. It's a cwm with a waterfall. Thirsty mosses thrive in its spray. Dense sessile oaks hide the floor. I pick one whose branches can hide me, away from everyone. There I rest and grieve.

★

She

Where would a man who's been betrayed go?

Out in the wilderness. Gwydion hunts him with his empathy and love. So I wander all over the region, using my mind to see how Lleu would perceive.

★

He

Better to be a dying eagle than an imaginary man, a character made up by others.

I hide because I hate the tricks that have kept me viable till now. Blodeuwedd saw through them be-cause she, like me, was kidnapped by Gwydion's plans. I love her still; she gave me the one way out, into reality.

210

★

She

When all else fails, turn to animals.

I stay with a peasant who has a pig of remarkable girth and health. At night, when she's let into the house, the heat from her glossy flesh keeps us cosy. I ask my host where the sow grazes. He doesn't know. I regard her eye, so human under its blonde eyelashes.

★

He

Except I'm finding it hard to die. My eye sees everything on the valley floor: voles and mice venturing out of cover, small flocks of songbirds feeding on insects in high branches, nuthatches creeping head-first down trunks…

I refuse them as food and feel the wind pass through me.

★

She

I follow the sow when she's let out of the house in the morning. She rushes into the woods and it's hard to keep up with her, she's so greedy.

I come to a hanging valley. In a grove one particular tree draws my attention and that of the sow. She's standing under it eating – what? I look closely. The tree is flush with scarlet and deep gold leaves and yes, they fall, but with them are meat and maggots. The sow is feasting on flesh. I crane my neck, look up and there, in the foliage, I see the dark brown of a bird. It's so emaciated that it's scarcely alive. I've found the wounded Lleu.

He

Nona, that's great that you've found Lleu, but I'm at the entrance to the interface.

She

This is the boy whose mother named him Light. He's living his autumn. No magic of mine could ever have avoided that.

He

Nona! It was staring us in the face all the time!

She

These falling gobbets of flesh are Lleu's flowers. Just as Math and I created Blodeuwedd, caused blossoms to become flesh, now Lleu is flowering into meat and I can't stop it.

He

The answer's in the characters that everyone forgot!

She

I must coax him down by talking. Can't use a spell, he's too weak. Besides, I think he's had enough of that. I'll tell him instead what he really is.

He

They've come together and have altered the rules of the game.

She

My darling, I see you as an eagle high in the top of the tree.

He

They are the context that make perfect sense of everything else.

Nona, I see Gwydion below me. His mouth is moving, but I don't understand what he's saying to me.

She

I see you Lleu, and though it's good to be here for a while, you don't belong in the forest.

He

Now I hear Gwydion's voice. It makes me home-sick. I hop down to hear more of its melody.

Nona, I need to tell you, everything we believed about this game is wrong.

She

I've hurt you. I've been too intent on having my own way. I beg that Lleu would come to my lap and forgive his uncle.

He

Oh, he speaks softly and I long to be close to this person who's so warm. What I've seen is true but cold.

She

Gwydion strikes his nephew with his wand and makes him a man again, though pitiful to see, thin and wasted.

And Campion opens his eyes and screams, Nona, we need to get off this ship. I've seen its core. The meat tree is eating us alive.

She

He's beside himself, so terrified that he makes no sense. He's raving.

So I sedate him and take his place.

★

He

I talk to Nona in my mind. I try to warn her but she goes ahead, reckless as ever.

She

The meat tree. Where Gwydion found the wounded Lleu. But he meant something else.

Gwydion and Lleu return to court for Lleu to recover his strength and to think how to take their revenge. Blodeuwedd and the hunter are living openly together in Lleu's own house. It's a scandal.

As Nona, I return to the tree and stand there alone, listening to the rustles in the grove. Somewhere a woodpecker drills. Moss grows on the northern side of the trunk, a vegetable shadow. The birds decide I'm worth ignoring and begin to sing. The glade settles down and I hear a small cry, a death in the underbrush. I begin to see.

First, a fawn-like pair of eyes that become a young man. Then another boy, just to his right, with the blonde eyelashes of a hog. Then a third with the startling yellow eyes of the wolf. I've no doubt that, had they so chosen, they could have remained invisible to me. The three boys born in the forest, Gwydion and Gilfaethwy's forgotten children: Hyddwn, Hychddwn and Bleiddwn.

And suddenly I think I know what Campion tried to tell me. It wasn't Math who was the Mastermind behind the VR games but these three sons. I'm looking at the centre of the game, its authors. Still silent, they look at me with curiosity, as if I were a strange animal.

I'm feeling uneasy and I don't know why. I saw these boys christened, so they should be no threat, nor even strangers to me and yet their stares are so alien that I feel my hands sweat. The boys seem to smell my fear and this brings tiny smiles to their mouths. One licks his lips. They circle me.

I should have waited for Campion. He'd know what to do.

He
Can't you see that these three shouldn't be here? They're monsters that look like children. Gwydion and Math's original sin is that they've mixed their stories with their own flesh and blood.

She
I step back and imagine how I appear to these boys. I see one breathe in, as if he's savouring my scent. It's terrifying.

He
That's it! You've got exactly the right connection. It's the imagination!

She

I must look strange to them, an interpolator from another age. A gatecrasher, someone who's changed the plot of their favourite story.

He

Yes, it's all to do with the plot!

She

Do they see me as on the side of the magicians who conjured them into being then left them alone? They move closer and I feel a rage – it must be from them – at being taken out of one realm in which they were happy, had parents and put into another where they were treated as orphans.

He

That's what they want, your empathy!

She

I look down at myself through their eyes and I'm startled to see how luscious my flesh looks, like orchid petals. My skin is translucent and I see my blood vessels throb with my goodness. I feel like prey.

He

That's it! They're hungry and you're their sport.

She

They're standing too close now and even if I tried, I couldn't break away from them.

He

Don't you see? They feed on your imagination. All the time we've been inside the game, we've been nothing but fuel. They used the plot to draw us in, like insects on the slippery ledge of a Venus flytrap.

She

We thought we were the investigators when, all the time, they were probing our minds.

He

Think literal, Nona, it's your only defence! The VR game has been one huge trap to lure us to the place where these three can use us completely.

She

They seem to be hypnotising me. I feel the pupils of my eyes dilate and I let them in. This is something like rape but more subtle, because they're feeding on… on - could it be… the story I've made up about them?

He

Think species of bird! The names of planets! Anything to take you away from the visions they're hunting.

She

I hear him! Think birds. Ah! Blackbird, sparrow, robin…

He

That's it! Carry on. What they hate is facts. Chaffinch!

She

Chaffinch! Uh… goldfinch! Woodpecker! Willow warbler…

He

They pull away from her and widen the circle. Tree creeper!

She

Heron! Barn owl! Crow!

He

Nona, take your chance and run!

★

She

When I get back, Campion's just stirring.

He

So, you've seen the interface now. What do you think?

She

That the game's not human.

He

It's not an Earth vessel at all. You tried to tell me, but I wouldn't listen.

She

It's come from much further afield, from outside this solar system. Maybe from somewhere like the Great

Attractor, or the Coma Cluster because you need that much time…

He
That's about three hundred million light years away…

She
Yes, long enough for the ship and crew to have evolved into something so strange we didn't recognise it.

He
It disguised itself, using what was in our own heads to look familiar.

She
You mean, it made itself look like our own ideas of a standard Earth ship of a certain period?

He
And that's the key. It used our own ideas.

She
But the VR stories. We didn't make those up.

He

No, they're part of the ship. The marriage of human beings with animals and plants…

She

So we can read that as a kind of parable of the vessel's history?

He

That's right. The ship's been travelling for millions of years. Since it set off there have been many generations of children born on board. They've grown up and had their own offspring time and time again. With such a small population, the gene pool must have become impoverished.

She

But where would they find more of their own species to mate with? We're not talking humans here, are we?

He

No, they must have come across some inhabited places – the odd colony or even stray ships, and bred with the species they found there, incorporated them into their genome.

She
You mean, like Gwydion and Gilfaethwy turning into various creatures in the forest?

He
Yes, it must have happened several times, and the story reflected it.

She
They must at some point have come across plants which then travelled with them.

He
And when two forms of life have so much time in a closed environment with each other – remember, we're talking millions of years – it's not strange to find… I can hardly think it.

She
That they evolved together?

He

I mean that they became a new species. An amalgam of the two.

She

Just like the offspring of Lleu and Blodeuwedd, if they'd had children? Are you saying that the VR is, as we suspected, the history of what happened to these people?

He

Yes, but as a people, not individuals. We were looking for the story of three persons, but the events described are far more epochal than that – what can happen on a voyage of three hundred million light years or more.

She

However vivid it was in VR, the story's over. The travellers died out and we just came across their ship, some aspects of which are still functioning. Big deal. Mystery solved. So, can't we just leave?

He

You try. You know that Mayday call. Do you think it went out?

She

Of course it did. It's all on automatic. The Department will be here for us any time now.

He

Go check the log. If what I think is right, we could be waiting a long time for a rescue vessel.

She

Here, look! I'll show you. Oh. That's odd. There's no sign of a Mayday. I know I sent it.

He

It's as I thought. Do one more thing for me. You know when you sealed the hatch between the vessels because the hull was pierced. Will you go and check its status?

She

But I can't do that without compounding the damage. The leak will get worse as I open the valve.

He

Trust me, Nona, just do as I say.

She

But… OK. I'll only do it if you stay in here, behind this atmos shield. I'll put on a breathing helmet and talk on the Joint Thought Channel, like before.

He

We don't seem to need it any more. But activate it if it makes you feel better.

She

Yes, it does. And you'll stay…?

He

Give me the shield.

She

Right, can you hear me? Good. I'm opening the lock and waiting for a sudden outrush of air any second.

Strange. I'm in the airlock now. I could have sworn the leak was just there. Where's it gone? I can't see it. Campion. There's no sign that anything ever pierced the hull in here. Look, I can take off my helmet and breathe. You can come out from behind the shield. Everything's normal.

He
Oh my God. Then it's true.

She
Isn't that good? That there's no damage?

He
For an intelligent woman you can be obtuse...

She
No need to insult me. I've got better things to be doing than being spoken to rudely by you.

He
Nona, don't you see what this means? There's no breach.

She
I must have been mistaken when I pulled you out of there.

He

And what about this wound in my chest? Is that an illusion?

She

No. Perhaps the seal slipped and is back in place now.

He

No, that isn't it. The ship itself repaired the hole in the hull.

She

But that's impossible. Ships don't heal.

He

But minds do. This whole ship is a mind. Anything can happen in three hundred million years. We've already established that the inhabitants interbred with plants. Take it one step further, Nona. What if the travellers on board combined with the ship, became their own transport?

She

You mean mind travel?

He

No, I mean literally. The people became their ship.

She

But that's crazy.

He

Is it? Evolution's a joker, can do strange things. Who'd have imagined a giraffe? In the same way as the voyagers married with plants, they made a physical bond with the ship and it allowed them to travel further than ever before. What substance do human beings have an infinite amount of?

She

Carbon?

He

No. I don't mean a chemical, an activity.

She

Ageing?

He

No, try again.

She
Bullshit?

He
No, but you're getting close. Imagination. As ubiquitous as light. If a ship could be driven by make-
believe then it would never ever run out of fuel, as
long as it had occupants.

She
But what if the original travellers all died? No
one's immortal.

He
Imagine if those in charge made the ship itself a
self-regulating system, so that it could lure other
creatures on board wherever it found them.

She
Like off the orbit of Mars.

He
And so it could get a new supply of fuel.

She

Especially if it didn't let them leave. Or prevented Maydays to other vessels. But I know I sent it.

He

No, you thought you did. Haven't we both been infected with this myth?

She

So the ship could travel on infinitely through the universe, incorporating other minds into itself where it found them?

He

Lured in by our curiosity and then by our love of a story. And all the time the ship was drawing life for itself from our explorations. Like a sundew. And that's how we've been caught.

She

That would explain my feeling of horror the first time we visited the VR. That wasn't a physical rape, it was mental.

He

The ship's been using our sensorium to feed itself and for us there's no way out. We've given it freely exactly what it wanted. Women of flowers… sex changes in a forest, we've had a fine old romp through the imagination. And it's taken it all and will never release us while there's a shred of mind in us that it can still use.

She

So that's why the forest boys drew close when I tried to imagine…

He

And once you stopped being empathetic they moved away.

She

But we could just leave.

He

I've already tried. The escape pod is jammed and none of the controls are answering my commands. We're being absorbed.

She

That explains… the rage of Blodeuwedd. I wonder
if she represents some being forced to be part of this
vessel against her will. If so, her distress has left its
mark on her character.

What are we going to do?

He

We probably shouldn't even be talking, as that itself
takes imagination.

She

We've got to talk or we'll both go mad.

Why don't we rest a while and try not to give the
vessel any fuel and see what that does?

He

I'm afraid it's far too late for that and just too difficult.
Have you ever tried not to think about something?
It makes it ten times more present and obtrusive. No.
There has to be another way out.

She

What if we do what they least expect and go back

into the VR? After all, the whole story is written in there, if we had eyes to see it. There may be some information that we've overlooked.

He
I don't know…

She
Well, I'll be damned if I'm waiting here till I go mad. If this vessel really is a cannibal ship, at least I want to use my own mind until the last moment. We know it uses us when we're asleep, I'd rather be active and see what comes.

He
You're right. We'll go in. But on one condition. That you take exactly the part I tell you to. And if I say run, you go hell for leather for the escape pod and leave, no matter what.

She
I promise.

He
Right. We have to go back into the forest.

She

I hated being by that tree. It's spooky.

He

Yes, but don't you see? It's the centre of everything.
The whole vessel's controlled by the interface with
the three lost boys.

  Are you ready?

She

I am. Hold my hand.

He

Right. Think of the meat tree.

She

But this doesn't look like the same place at all. This
is... I don't know what. Look at those wires going
into... no!

He

It's something like flesh. They look like veins. I can
see them pulsing. This is still the meat tree but now
we're seeing what it really is – where the spaceship
merged with human bodies, became something else.
It's evolution.

She

So we're to be next? What are we supposed to do?

He

Go back to the story. It's been our guide so far.

She

Why did Lleu come here, to the meat tree, at his moment of crisis? I'd have thought he'd want to escape the story that had failed to give him a wife and nearly killed him.

He

But don't you see that Lleu knows he's entirely a creature of illusion? He could have been like the three lost boys. They've hardly any human biography, but they know what they are. Lleu would be less than nothing, were it not for his uncles' sleight-of-hand. Strip that away and he's an emaciated bird of prey, being fed on by a sow.

She

Look! Some action! Back at the court. Math and Gwydion in consultation with Lleu. All three are demanding recompense from the hunter and Blodeuwedd.

He

I'll take the part of Lleu. You stay and observe.

She

But I want to help and I'm good at this.

He

You promised to do as I said. This way it's safer. I'll tell you what's happening as we go. I don't want you taking on any roles until we know more.

Lleu demands to be avenged on the hunter.

First they deal with Blodeuwedd. When she and her ladies hear that Math is coming, they flee. They're so afraid that they run looking backwards and all of them fall in a lake, where they drown. Except for Blodeuwedd.

She

I'm taking her part!

He

Nona! I told you not to do it!

She

Too late, I'm in. And I'm being cursed.

No, it's not drowning they have in mind for me, but turning me into a bird. My maids turned their faces round like an owl's to look over their shoulders. My heart is at the end of its passion. I'm still beautiful with a beak, and a splay of feathers as if a wind blew constantly into my eyes and ruffled my feathers into a face. I have talons.

I try to laugh because compared to being a plant this is up the evolutionary ladder! But it comes out mournful. I flee the day because what they give me is shame and blood at night. Remorse is always hunting and finding its prey.

He

For Lleu and Gwydion and Math are men of honour. So is the hunter.

She

Campion! Listen to Blodeuwedd. It's you who should get out. I've got to tell you…

He

Your voice has turned soft, I can hardly hear you.
Gwydion demands that the hunter stand in the spot
where Lleu was tricked and receive the same blow.

She

The reason they made me an owl…

He

The hunter asks if any of his men will take the hit on
his behalf.

She

Is because I'm a master bird of prey. Don't you see?

He

But nobody will.

She

The ship is entering another phase, with another
species. The story determines what the ship can do
physically. It's turning overtly predatory!

He

So the hunter prepares himself to stand where Lleu

balanced beside the river.

She

This is so hard to follow. Till now, the ship wanted us for our imagination. But this intelligence is looking for bodies in which to give birth to their ideas. That's why they've been after us since we first went into VR. The fruit of this tree is always meat and more meat – the babies born from incest. A woman – fresh meat – made of the flesh of flowers. Now that tree is hungry.

Campion! Listen! From now on the meat tree will eat us alive! Not only our minds but our bodies as well! It's time to leave.

He

You go, that's an order. I'll find a point where I can distract them.

She

It's too late for that. I'm switching roles.

He

Don't you dare! The hunter asks if he may hold a

stone as a shield before him. I say, 'Yes. I will not refuse you that.'

She

I'll be the hunter and take the blow.

He

What was that? Say again? I told you get out, and use the pod.

    I take my javelin, balance it on my shoulder.

She

He can't see who's behind the stone.

He

I think like light and ignore all objects. I concentrate with a hatred so sharp I can place my spear with precision in between molecules of air…

She

The hunter acts out of instinct alone. His mind is clear as the sky above him. There's not a shred of fantasy in it. He's a man who's willing to pay for his actions, who understands pain is never touched by magic. I stand here for Campion, the first real gesture in this whole game.

THE MEAT TREE

He

Time slows down, and I see the blade vibrate as it flies. It parts the slate like a laser through dust and finds its mark.

She

The spear finds my heart like a new love. I feel the rhythm of my blood as it pumps out of my wound. As I fall, I catch Campion's eye.

He

My God, it's Nona!

She

The meat tree shakes as I become its fruit. Everything concentrates on me as the sweet juice runs over.

He

She's wearing a flower of red on her breast and, with her blood, she tells me to go. I run.

She

Every grievance, every form of justice played out in the game needs this moment of death. No tricks with birds, no transformations. Just falling and bleeding.

He

I fire up the pod and it works this time. The ship is distracted.

She

Imagination is all very well, but it requires a body, which is its better part.

He

The engine is sluggish, as if it were held by millions of tiny plant tendrils. Full throttle and the tiny ship moves away from the shipwreck.

She

The metal was cold but now it burns.

He

The engines roar, make way.

She

Darkness falls on my face, like an owl.

He

What will I tell them when I get back? We'll find no body. Nona will be changed beyond all explanation.

I'm away! And as I leave, I hear her:

Campion, remember that you weren't alone inside this story. That you and I were married, me to light, you to flowers. Look to the skies and tell me that it's better to see than it is to be seen.

I feel her mind. Nona! So many illusions that the blow of the real…

… is saving.

I've seen a rogue cell of alien imagination that consumed a living girl. I myself scarcely survived. And now what? A life alone on Mars surface? Like Lleu, I shall have my domain but rule alone. I'll live in the loneliness of night.

No, Campion, you'll have your witness always. And your justice.

The stars are in turmoil, light never dies.

The Fourth Branch of the *Mabinogion*
Blodeuwedd

Math was the lord of Gwyneth and Pryderi of land to the south. Math could only live if his feet were in the lap of a virgin, except when there was a war.

Goewin, his footholder, was the most beautiful maiden in the land and Math's nephew, Gilfaethwy desired her. So Gilfaethwy's brother, Gwydion, the best storyteller in the world, engineered a war with the south and while the king was away Gilfaethwy raped Goewin. When Math discovered this he married Goewin as recompense. He punished his nephews by turning them into animals for three years, deer for the first year, then boar, then wolves. He forced them to breed and have offspring, whom he fostered. The three boys were named Hyddwn, Hychddwn and Bleiddwn.

When the punishment was over, Gwydion pro-posed his sister Aranrhod as Math's new footholder. Math asked her to step over his magic wand but when she did so she left behind a yellow-haired boy and something else that Gwydion took and hid in a trunk in his room. Later he heard a cry and found a small boy, whom he took to a nursemaid. By the age of four the boy was as strong as an eight year old and Gwydion took him to Aranrhod. Furious, she cursed him to have no name unless she gave him one; but Gwydion tricked her into naming him Lleu Law Gyffes (the fair-haired one with the skilful hand).

Then Aranrhod swore Lleu would have no weapons unless she gave them to him, but again Gwydion tricked her. Finally his mother swore Lleu would never have a wife from the race that is on this earth. But Gwydion and Math made Lleu a wife out of the flowers of oak, broom and meadowsweet; they called her Blodeuwedd.

Math gave Lleu some land to rule, but while her husband was away Blodeuwedd met a huntsman; they fell in love and plotted to kill Lleu. Blodeuwedd asked her husband how he could die, saying she was worried for his safety. He told her he could only be killed by a spear that had taken a year to make while people were at mass on Sundays. Even then he would have to be standing under a roof by a river with one foot on a bath and one on a goat.

Blodeuwedd told this to the huntsman, Gronw Pebr, and a year later asked her husband to show her what he meant. When he did so Gronw threw the spear at him; Lleu screamed, turned into an eagle and flew away. He hid but Gwydion found the eagle at the top of a tree, and when it shook itself worms and rotten flesh fell from it. Gwydion enticed it down and changed it back into a man. When he was well, Lleu asked Math for recompense. Gwydion found Blodeuwedd and turned her into an owl. Lleu demanded the huntsman let him throw a spear at him, Gronw asked for a stone to shield him but the spear broke the stone and killed him. Lleu reclaimed his lands, afterwards becoming Lord of Gwynedd.

Synopsis by Penny Thomas:
for the full story see *The Mabinogion, A New Translation* by Sioned Davies (Oxford World's Classics, 2007).

Afterword

I've been wanting to work with the Blodeuwedd myth since I saw a certain tree one autumn when I was twenty-two. It was in America and the only way I had to describe the incandescent fall of its leaves was to say it was Lleu, an eagle perched in the branches and dropping his bright flesh into the dirt.

Nothing came of this image until I was given the chance to retell one of the *Mabinogion* by Seren Books. I've known the myths since I was a child. In junior school, we put on a show of *Culhwch ac Olwen*, in which I played Culhwch and my mother gave me a row for biting my nails during the wedding scene with my consort, Olwen.

So, how to retell a story whose lyrical potential is obvious, with the woman made from flowers its most popular motif? I hesitated to make the creation of Blodeuwedd the centre of the story because she appears at the end of a long sequence of previous events. The idea of genetic engineering was suggestive but I didn't want to make the tale a parable about the folly of man's tampering with nature because the life of the whole myth seemed to me to lie elsewhere.

The Fourth Branch of the *Mabionogion* contains rape, incest, bestiality, miracle births and murder. Its characters shape-shift, give birth to animal offspring. It's a tale about the limit of magic and the ways in which it bumps up against forces that will not be charmed into compliance with men's plans. The story as a whole, I believe, is about the imagination.

I've been a fan of science fiction since I was a teenager and have often noted how myths find a natural place in such writing. So I resolved to try and tell the Blodeuwedd story on a spaceship. I read a lot of sci-fi in preparation, ranging from William Gibson's *Neuromancer* to Alan Moore's graphic novel *Swamp Thing*. I thought that evolution would have a part in the story, so I found a copy of Charles Darwin's *The Power of Movement in Plants,* where he draws diagrams of the winding movements made by all vegetation as it follows the sun. My plant, Blodeuwedd, though, was going to travel much further in her voyage to Mars orbit.

Although much of the Fourth Branch is taken up with the rites of passage which Lleu requires in order to become a man, the main character of the story is Gwydion, his uncle. Gwydion is not only a wizard but also a storyteller. The early parts of the myth are devoted to his education. After he helps his brother commit rape, their brother, Math, punishes them both. The penance is to be changed into animals and be forced to breed with each other and bear young. Gwydion is to learn literally what it is to behave like an animal.

This book was written while I was a Fellow at the Stanford Humanities Center in California. While I was there, I met Joan Roughgarden, whose book *Evolution's Rainbow* (University of California Press, 2009) argues that:

the most common body form among plants and in perhaps half the animal kingdom is for an individual to be both male and female at the same, or at different times in its life.

I found this fascinating because it gave a biological basis for the education of Gwydion. The great moment for him comes after he's done his utmost for Lleu, has tricked Aranrhod into giving him a name, arms and a wife. Gwydion follows the sow to the meat tree and sees the damage that his plotting has done to Lleu. Faced with the possibility of Lleu dying, Gwydion has to rethink everything.

I've heard poets argue that today poetry is a force that opposes technology. I believe that poetry itself is one of the earliest technologies and that the imagination is a form of virtual reality. I wanted to explore the way in which a certain kind of Celtic mythology is used in computer games and to deploy the convention to make a broader point about the imagination. I particularly wanted to look at the shadow side of the creative mind, the way in which it can consume as well as generate. Every writer is a meat tree of sorts.

I owe a debt to David Grossman's retelling of the Samson myth, *Lions' Honey* (Canongate, 2007). His brilliant critical reading of the story shed some light for me on the circumstances of Lleu's betrayal by Blodeuwedd. Why was he so willing to give her the secret of how he could be killed? Like Samson, perhaps, Lleu, who was rejected by his mother, felt the need to:

> relive again and again, the experience of being betrayed again and again, the experience of being betrayed by those close to him, the compulsion to re-enact, over and over, that primal event of being handed over to strangers, of being given up.

The *Mabinogion* as a whole give an extraordinarily powerful glimpse into the medieval mind as it explored ways of living and their limitations. My code is that of being a writer and I couldn't help but see the losses, as well as the gains which that vocation requires. It may demand a certain kind of solitude but when entered into fully, there's a dialogue with the self, which is much wider than the ego. This is a conversation with other people and minds, even though those with whom we speak – other story-tellers among them – aren't physically present. This is a tree, after all, whose branches are still bearing fruit and on which new leaves can never feel lonely.

Acknowledgements

I'd like to thank Professor Catherine McKenna of Harvard University for taking the time to discuss the Fourth Branch of the *Mabinogion* with me and for her insights. I'm also indebted to Xandra Clark for her comments on the manuscript.

The book was written while I was Joint Sica/Stanford Humanities Center Fellow in the Arts and Humanities and I'm deeply grateful to both institutions.

p 23 Quotations from Campion's training manual are taken from Philip Robert Harris, *Living and Working in Space: Human Behavior, Culture and Organization* (Praxis, 1996).

pp 125-28, 141 Quotations are taken from Sioned Davies' translation of *The Mabinogion* (Oxford World's Classics, 2007), p 55. I have followed Professor Davies' spellings of proper names with one exception – Blodeuwedd – which is the spelling with which I was brought up.

pp 152-53 *ibid*, p 58.

pp 179-80, 201-2 The information about perfumes comes from Nigel Groom, *The Perfume Handbook* (London, 1992). I'm grateful to Richard Mabey for drawing my attention to it.

pp 199-200 Some of the language to describe Blodeuwedd at night is taken from Charles Darwin, *The Power of Movement in Plants* (New York, 1966), p 106.

pp 207-8 Some of the language used to describe the lovemaking of Blodeuwedd and the hunter is drawn from Maurice Maeterlinck, *The Intelligence of Flowers*, tr Philip Mosley (State of New York Press, 2005), p 22.

OWEN SHEERS
WHITE RAVENS

"Hauntingly imaginative..." – Dannie Abse

Two stories, two different times, but the thread of an ancient tale runs through the lives of twenty-first-century farmer's daughter Rhian and the mysterious Branwen... Wounded in Italy, Matthew O'Connell is seeing out WWII in a secret government department spreading rumours and myths to the enemy. But when he's given the bizarre task of escorting a box containing six raven chicks from a remote hill farm in Wales to the Tower of London, he becomes part of a story over which he seems to have no control.

Based on the Mabinogion story 'Branwen, Daughter of Llyr', *White Ravens* is a haunting novella from an award-winning writer.

Owen Sheers is the author of two poetry collections, *The Blue Book* and *Skirrid Hill* (both Seren); a Zimbabwean travel narrative, *The Dust Diaries* (Welsh Book of the Year 2005); and a novel, *Resistance*, shortlisted for the Writers' Guild Best Book Award. *A Poet's Guide to Britain* is the accompanying anthology to Owen's BBC 4 series.

RUSSELL CELYN JONES
THE NINTH WAVE

"A brilliantly-imagined vision of the near future...
one of his finest achievements." – Jonathan Coe

Pwyll, a young Welsh ruler in a post-oil world, finds his inherited
status hard to take. And he's never quite sure how he's drawn into
murdering his future wife's fiancé, losing his only son and
switching beds with the king of the underworld. In this bizarrely
upside-down, medieval world of the near future, life is cheap and
the surf is amazing; but you need a horse to get home again down
the M4.

Based on the Mabinogion story 'Pwyll, Lord of Dyfed', *The Ninth
Wave* is an eerie and compelling mix of past, present and future.
Russell Celyn Jones swops the magical for the psychological, the
courtly for the post-feminist and goes back to Swansea Bay to
complete some unfinished business.

Russell Celyn Jones is the author of six novels. He has won the
David Higham Prize, the Society of Authors Award, and the
Weishanhu Award (China). He is a regular reviewer for several
national newspapers and is Professor of Creative Writing at
Birkbeck College, London.

NIALL GRIFFITHS
THE DREAMS OF MAX & RONNIE

There's war and carnage abroad and Iraq-bound squaddie Ronnie is out with his mates 'forgetting what has yet to happen'. He takes something dodgy and falls asleep for three nights in a filthy hovel where he has the strangest of dreams, watching the tattooed tribes of modern Britain surrounding a grinning man playing war games.

Meanwhile gangsta Max is fed up with life in his favourite Cardiff nightclub, Rome, and chases a vision of the perfect woman in far-flung parts of his country. But as Max loses his heart, his followers fear he may be losing his touch.

Niall Griffiths' retellings of two dream myths from the medieval Welsh Mabinogion cycle reveal an astonishingly contemporary and satirical resonance. Arthurian legend merges with its twenty-first century counterpart in a biting commentary on leadership, conflict and the divisions in British society.

Niall Griffiths was born in Liverpool in 1966, studied English, and now lives and works in Aberystwyth. His novels include *Grits*, *Sheepshagger, Kelly and Victor* and *Stump*, which won Wales Book of the Year, and *Runt*. His non-fiction includes *Real Aberystwyth* and *Real Liverpool*. He also writes reviews, radio plays and travel pieces.